WITHDRAWN

MARGI PREUS

AMULET BOOKS ■ NEW YORK

Library of Congress Cataloging-in-Publication Data

Preus, Margi.
Shadow on the mountain : a novel inspired by the true adventures of a
wartime spy / by Margi Preus.
p. cm.
Summary: In Nazi-occupied Norway, fourteen-year-old Espen joins the
resistance movement, graduating from deliverer of illegal newspapers to
courier and spy.
Includes bibliographical references (p.).
ISBN 978-1-4197-0424-6 (alk. paper)
1. World War, 1939–1945—Underground movements—Norway—Juvenile
fiction. 2. Norway—History—German occupation, 1940–1945—Juvenile
fiction. [1. World War, 1939–1945—Underground movements—Norway—
Fiction. 2. Norway—History—German occupation, 1940–1945—Fiction.
3. Spies—Fiction.] I. Title.
PZ7.P92434Sh 2012
[Fic]—dc23
2012015623

Text copyright © 2012 Margi Preus
Illustration © 2012 Yuko Shimizu
Maps by Sara Corbett
Book design by Chad W. Beckerman and Sara Corbett

Printed and bound in U.S.A.
10 9 8 7 6 5 4 3 2 1

Amulet Books are available at special discounts when purchased
in quantity for premiums and promotions as well as fundraising or
educational use. Special editions can also be created to specification. For
details, contact specialsales@abramsbooks.com or the address below.

ABRAMS
THE ART OF BOOKS SINCE 1949

115 West 18th Street
New York, NY 10011
www.abramsbooks.com

In loving memory
of my parents,
Chris and Dorothy
Preus, with thanks
for their stories

Shadows made the mountains dark, and you, you didn't find the way.

—LINE FROM "SYNNØVE'S SONG," LYRICS BY BJ. BJØRNSON

Approximations of the Pronunciation of Names and Words

Aksel	AK-SEL	
bestemor	BEST-EH-MOOR	GRANDMOTHER
draug	DROWG	WATER CREATURE
Espen	ES-PEN	
far	FAR	FATHER
fjord	FYORD	AN INLET OF THE SEA BETWEEN HIGH CLIFFS
Gust	GOOST	
Haakon	HAWK-ON	
hei	HI	HELLO
hird	HEERD	NORWEGIAN NAZI STORM TROOPERS
Hjalmer	HYAL-MER	
huldre	HUL-DRA	TROLL HAG
Hvepsen	VEP-SEN	*THE WASP*

Ingrid	ING-GRID	
ja	YA	YES
Jens	YENS	
Jotunheimen	YO-TUN-HEIM-EN	LAND OF THE GIANTS
Kjell	SHELL	
krone/kroner	CRONE/CRO-NER	CROWN/CROWNS: NORWEGIAN MONEY
Leif	LIFE	
Lilleby	LIL-LE-BEE	
Mor	MOOR	MOTHER
nei	NIE	NO
nisselue	NISS-EH-LU-EH	RED STOCKING HAT
Ole	OH-LEH	
Per	PEAR	
Ragnarok	RAHG-NA-ROK	FINAL DESTRUCTION IN NORSE MYTHOLOGY
Solveig	SOL-VAY	
Tante Marie	TAHN-TEH MA-REE	AUNT MARIE
tusen takk	TOOS-EN TUCK	A THOUSAND THANKS
vær så god	VAIR SO GO	BE SO GOOD; HELP YOURSELF

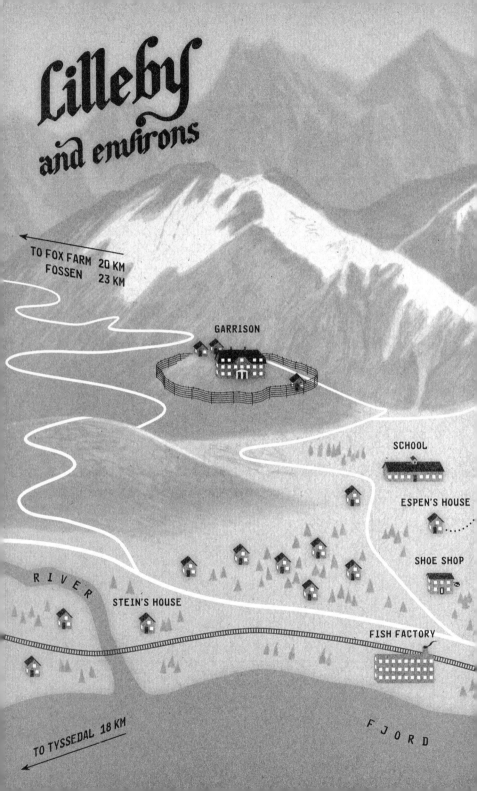

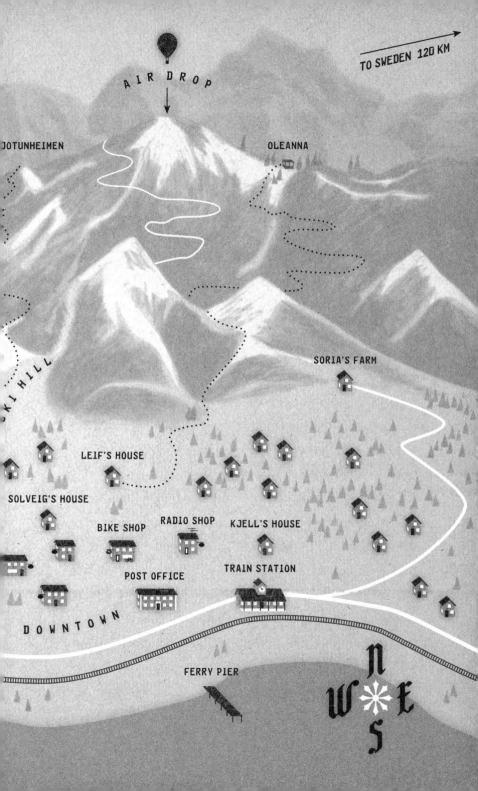

Prologue

J ust before dawn on April 9, 1940, Nazi Germany invaded Norway, a neutral and peace-loving country of only three million people. The Norwegians were completely unprepared for the onslaught of eight hundred aircraft, ten thousand advance troops, and almost the entire German navy. By noon, the Wehrmacht had taken control of Oslo, two major airports, and the most important coastal cities. The Norwegians scrambled to organize a military response, and for a few desperate weeks, aided by a small force of Allied troops, they put up a valiant but ultimately futile fight.

Some members of the government, including Vidkun Quisling, head of the Norwegian Nazi party, welcomed the Germans. Upon the invasion, Quisling quickly deposed the sitting government and declared himself prime minister.

In May, the Allied forces withdrew from Norway, and in early June, King Haakon and other members of the government left Norway for England and the Norwegian military disbanded. Nazi Germany was now occupying the country and was fully in control.

Or *were* they?

The occupying Germans had expected Norwegians to welcome them as their protectors against the Soviet Union. Fair-haired, blue-eyed, tall and fit, the Norwegians embodied the ideal of the Aryan race, which, according to Hitler, was destined to be the master race, and the Germans were unprepared for the hostility they encountered. An organized resistance formed almost immediately, including underground military groups (Milorg), civilian groups (Civorg), and intelligence units (XU), with a Coordinating Committee (KK) overseeing the common struggle. The movement was aided by a new British military branch called the SOE (Special Operatives Executive). But even ordinary Norwegians, young and old, found myriad ways of resisting. Despite an enormous military presence—one German soldier for every eight Norwegians—and in spite of the military's brutal methods, so effective was this resistance that President Franklin D. Roosevelt was inspired to say to the American people:

If there is anyone who still wonders why this war is being fought, let him look to Norway. If there is anyone who has any delusions that this war could have been averted, let him look to Norway; and if there is anyone who doubts the democratic will to win, again I say, let him look to Norway.

1940–1941

THE NORWEGIANS' INTELLIGENCE IS A LITTLE SLOW,
AND THEY ARE SUSPICIOUS OF FOREIGNERS; THEREFORE,
THE BENEVOLENT GERMAN MUST NOT LOSE HIS TEMPER BUT
TAKE MATTERS CALMLY . . . IT IS BETTER TO EXPLAIN
THINGS TO THEM IN A SIMPLE, MATTER-OF-FACT WAY
OR, STILL BETTER, TO ADOPT A PLAYFUL TONE.

—INSTRUCTIONS GIVEN TO GERMAN
SOLDIERS SERVING IN NORWAY

On the Road to the Fox Farm

gainst the blue-black mountains, Espen's bicycle was just a tiny moving speck. Far below the road, the river pulsed and rushed, swollen with rain and snowmelt. The sun had long ago slipped away, leaving just a thin fringe of light glimmering along the ragged edge of the western mountains. *The dangerous time of day,* his grandmother would have said, *the time of day the trolls come out.*

Head down, straining forward over the handlebars, Espen felt his heart pump in rhythm with his legs. The muscles in his arms and legs burned, his heart beat furiously, and, ridiculously, his stomach was growling. He was always hungry. But how could he be hungry *now?*

"Cream cake," he said aloud, savoring the words as if eating them, feeling the sweet, silky "cream" melt on his tongue, then biting into the delicious sponginess of "cake." He shouldn't think about it, he scolded himself. He shouldn't think about anything but going faster.

A car drove up behind him and slowed. He pedaled harder, sweating under the rucksack on his back. *Why don't they pass?* he wondered. By the car's puttering he could tell it was not fitted with a wood-burning engine, which the Norwegians were required to drive. It burned petrol, so it had to be Germans.

Don't look over your shoulder, he told himself. *If they want to stop you, they can stop you. Just don't think about it. Think about something else. But not cream cake.*

He wondered what was happening at home. His father would still be at the train station, working his usual long hours. His mother would be worrying about them both, glancing out the window one last time before pulling the blackout curtains closed. His sister, Ingrid, would be up in her room, probably scribbling in her diary.

The car pulled up alongside Espen, and he glanced at it. He felt a rivulet of sweat run down his back. The car was full of German soldiers. The driver waved at him to stop, and Espen did, standing with one foot on the ground, the other resting on the pedal. Right away, his glasses fogged up. He took them off and cleaned the lenses with his shirt. Then he gave one last thought to his family, hoping that whatever happened next would not put their lives in jeopardy.

One of the soldiers got out of the car and held out his hand. "*Ausweiss, bitte,*" he said.

Espen dug in his pocket and handed the soldier his identity card. The soldier, Espen noticed, smelled clean. Like soap.

"Where are you going?" the soldier asked.

"To visit my uncle. He lives near Fossen."

"What is the purpose of your visit?"

"Just a visit," Espen said.

The soldier raised an eyebrow, so Espen continued. "My uncle's been ill, and my mother's worried about him. He doesn't have a telephone, so I said I would go check on him." Espen resisted the urge to go on with his story. *Keep it simple,* he remembered Mr. Henriksen telling him. *If they ask you questions, keep it simple. Don't rattle on.*

The soldier shone his flashlight in Espen's face. "Out so late?"

"I had soccer practice," Espen said. "We have a big match coming up. I got a late start."

"How old are you?"

"Fourteen," Espen said.

The soldier nodded at Espen's rucksack. "What's in there?" he asked in not-very-good Norwegian.

"Jam," Espen said.

The soldier extended his arm to take the rucksack.

Espen handed it over and tried not to watch the man's face as he opened it. Instead, he shifted his gaze to the car. He could see the bored faces of the soldiers and one who turned his head. But not fast enough. Espen had seen who it was. Kjell.

They hadn't done much together lately, but it used to be that he and Kjell had spent every waking moment with each other. Just last April, after the Germans invaded, they had spent the next days with their ears pressed to the radio and their eyes on the roads, listening, watching, waiting. And spying.

~—#—•

The April day the German army reached their valley, Espen had followed Kjell along paths worn into the snow, leading up the hillside through the woods. All along the path rose columns of silent fir trees, their damp trunks reminding Espen of the woolen coats of the German soldiers. He half expected one to lunge out at them, bayonet flashing.

"Aren't you scared?" He panted a little, hurrying after Kjell.

"Nei!" Kjell said. "It's fun!" He turned around, grinning.

Kjell was never afraid of anything. He went toward danger, not away from it. That's what Espen's mother said, anyway, and why she told Espen that he had to "keep a level head" when they were together. She would have clobbered them both, Espen thought, if she knew what they were doing at that moment.

"I have to be back before dark," Espen said. "Mor decided that she is taking Ingrid and me to stay with relatives in the country, to get away from the fighting."

"Just this one last mission before you go, then, right?" Kjell said.

The trees had thinned as they reached a higher elevation, and the boys dashed from one to the next.

"This mission will be better than when you had us

prowling around in the woods looking for the king," Kjell said. "That was a bust!"

"I swear, the whole royal family was hiding out around here somewhere," Espen said. "They're long gone by now. At least, I hope so."

"Shh!" Kjell held up his hand.

The dull roar of an airplane echoed against the mountainside.

"German fighter!" Kjell cried. "They strafe anything that moves! Run!"

But Espen felt as weak as if he were in a bad dream, as if his legs would not carry him.

Kjell grabbed his arm and dragged him under the cover of a cluster of birch trees.

The plane flew over and away, and the boys got up, brushed off the snow, and moved on, leaving the trees for the open, windswept hillside. Kjell flopped down, slithering snakelike on his belly, with Espen following him closely. They crept behind a large boulder where they could see but not be seen.

Kjell held a finger to his lips, and slowly, carefully, the two boys peeked over the rock.

In the darkening valley below, a procession of motorcycles, trucks, tanks, cars, horse-drawn wagons, marching soldiers, and soldiers on horseback snaked along the winding mountain road. The last rays of sunlight glanced off the barrels of the soldiers' guns, their polished leather boots, and even, it seemed, off the brass buttons on their long gray-green coats.

Espen's breath caught in his throat. Their sheer numbers and firepower made his stomach churn, but there was something more. Maybe it was a trick of light or the dusk, or maybe it was the fast hike up the mountainside that had made him dizzy, but for just a moment it looked to him as if the entire army was not coming from around a bend in the road but pouring endlessly out of a cleft in the earth. He thought of something his great-grandmother had told him: that sometimes, at dawn or at dusk, a crack opened up in the earth out of which the people of the underworld could climb and into which the people of the upper world—"our world," she had said—could slide.

He shivered.

"Cold?" Kjell asked.

"There sure are a lot of them, aren't there?" Espen said.

"They're like a well-oiled machine," Kjell said. "So precise. And so many! And no one can say the Wehrmacht isn't disciplined! Our so-called troops are nothing but a ragtag bunch of ill-trained misfits—no uniforms, old hunting rifles for weapons—"

"But lots of courage," Espen said.

"Maybe so. But still no match for them." Kjell nodded at the never-ending columns of soldiers below.

"If I had a rifle, I could pick off a couple right now," Espen said.

"That would not be the smartest thing you've ever done."

"I suppose not."

"Look at that one there." Kjell pointed at an officer astride a spirited white horse.

Espen glanced at Kjell. His eyes were shining as he gazed at the horse prancing this way and that, its sides gleaming as if polished.

"Kjell," Espen said, "you know how the huldre can look like a beautiful maiden from the front, but in the back she has a long tail she keeps tucked into her skirt?"

"We're not troll hunting anymore, Espen," Kjell said.

"And how a water troll can transform himself into a beautiful jewel or even into a powerful white horse?" Espen continued.

"This isn't a game," Kjell said. "This is for real."

"I know!" Espen said. "I know. But, Kjell, once you climb onto that horse's back, you are in its power."

"What are you talking about?"

"It can take you away, and you can't do anything about it."

———

"You are wrong about the contents of your rucksack," the soldier said.

Espen was jolted back to the dark road, the idling car, and the soldier standing in front of him holding his backpack. "What's that?" he asked.

"I said that you are wrong about what is in here."

"Oh?" Espen tried unsuccessfully to keep his voice from cracking.

"This," the German said, holding up a jar, "is *jelly*"—he smiled—"not *jam*."

"Ah," Espen said, "I always get that wrong."

"See?" the soldier shone his flashlight beam through the jar so the jelly glowed a jewel-like red. "See how clear it is? Jelly is clear—like this—and jam has in it the fruit pulp." His Norwegian was terrible.

The soldier handed him back the rucksack, nodded politely, and went back to the car. As he moved past, Espen noticed the soap smell again. A moment later, the car puttered away. Espen could not help but smile. When the soldiers were well down the road, he thumbed his nose at the whole lot of them and let out a little howl of glee. "You were outfoxed!" he yelled at the distant taillights. Then he waited for a few moments until his legs stopped trembling before climbing back onto his bike.

The valley narrowed, and waterfalls plunged off the ever steeper mountainsides into the river below. Still fifteen kilometers to go. Darkness had descended; it seemed to sharpen the smell of fall, sharp and yeasty like something baking. Sour rye bread, maybe.

Espen tried to keep himself from thinking about what could go wrong and decided to think instead about the upcoming soccer match. For the first time in as long as anyone could remember, his team had a shot—a real shot—at the championship. He wondered if Kjell would show up for the game. He hadn't been at practices for a long time now. If he came, Espen could ask him why he'd been in a car with German soldiers.

The steep climb had made Espen overheat. He stopped and took off his windcheater, which he stuffed into his rucksack. Although he couldn't see it, he could hear the roar of a distant waterfall and the wind high in the pine boughs. Behind those sounds was the deep and abiding silence of the mountains. The silence of secrets being kept. Plenty of secrets.

Like the one he carried with him right now: two sheets of folded paper, the outside of which read, *Growing Potatoes in Your Garden*.

He climbed back onto his bike and resumed pedaling.

"Be careful how you carry it," his teacher had said when he'd given the paper to him after all his classmates had left the room that afternoon. "Best to keep it well hidden. There may be German patrols out. Seems they're looking for—"

Suddenly, he was speaking rather loudly, ". . . a good way to grow potatoes in your own garden."

Espen looked up. One of his classmates had entered the

room. *She walked over to her desk and picked up a book, then waved at them and went back out.*

"Don't tell anyone what you're doing," Mr. Henriksen had said. "Not your sister, not your classmates—not even Kjell."

So he hadn't told anyone. Not his sister, not his classmates, not even his parents. And not Kjell. He hadn't even seen Kjell. Not for days, at least.

When Espen and his sister had returned to Lilleby in June after their stay in the country, Kjell was . . . different. It had been less than two months, but he had changed. But then, everything had changed. The Germans had taken over Norway, and nothing was the same as before.

Now there were so many secrets. Kjell must have a secret, too, Espen thought. Otherwise, why was he in that car?

The Fox Farm

Espen's tires crunched on the gravel of the driveway into the fox farm. He glanced around for the glint of eyes. Did the foxes just run around loose? He wasn't sure.

Two empty milk bottles on the front porch, Mr. Henriksen had said, was the sign that it was safe to go inside.

The house was filled with heaven: the fragrance of waffles cooking on a griddle. Espen's glasses steamed up immediately, and he took them off to clean them. When he put them back on, he saw first a head of red hair and then the rest of the small, round woman who had appeared from the kitchen door.

"Were you followed?" she asked.

Espen shook his head. "I was stopped, though," he said. "They searched my backpack."

"Really!" she said. "And . . . ?"

"There was nothing in it except, um, jelly."

"Good boy," she said. She brushed a wisp of hair away, then held out her hand. "Nice to meet you. Call me 'Tante Marie.'"

Espen shook her hand and said, "My name is—"

"Ssst!" she hissed. "Your code name?"

"I don't have one," he said.

"Well, we'll have to fix that!" she said.

A code name! Espen thought. His stomach buzzed a little with excitement.

"Now, then, give me what you brought," Tante Marie said.

Espen reached down and slid the folded papers from one of his long woolen stockings.

"Clever boy!" she said. "Now, come in."

Espen stepped into the kitchen, where he couldn't help but notice the steam rising from a waffle griddle.

"It's just about growing potatoes in your garden," Espen said, watching her face.

Tante Marie cocked an eyebrow, then smiled. "OK," she said, "you know it's more than that."

"Still," he said, "it's only news!"

Tante Marie sucked in her breath with an inward "*Ja*" as she perused the paper. "Did you ever think that 'only news' would get to be so precious?" She clucked her tongue as she read aloud the main points of the stories: "Reichskommissar Terboven has 'deposed' the king and the government and dissolved all political parties but the Nazi party . . . Norwegian Nazi storm troopers attacked and beat up a teacher and his students at a school in Oslo . . . In Trondheim, a student was beaten because he wouldn't put up a poster for the Nazis . . . Let's see," she went on. "Our well-respected Dr. Scharffenberg addressed the university students recently. He said, 'Let the Nazis know that Norway's youth will defend freedom and independence no matter the cost to us all.'"

Espen cleared his throat. "I would . . . I could do something to help," he said.

Tante Marie's eyes flickered over him like small blue flames. "What do you propose?"

"Whatever is needed," he replied. "I could do it. I'm quite fit. I can bicycle quite fast, if need be."

Tante Marie pursed her lips and said, "Well . . . sit down here."

He sat at the table in front of a platter heaped with—

"Waffles!" Espen exclaimed. "I must be dreaming!" He glanced around but didn't see anyone else. "All for me?"

She laughed. "Have you been a good boy?"

"Hmm . . ." Espen remembered that he had swiped the jelly from his mother's pantry. "Not especially."

She clucked her tongue but put a couple of waffles onto a plate and slid it toward him. "*Vær så god,*" she said. "Help yourself."

He marveled at the food for a moment. "Where did you get eggs?" he asked.

"I know some hens," Tante Marie said.

"I have some jelly!" Espen took the jar out of his rucksack and snapped off the lid. He hadn't realized it would come in so handy, and he was glad his uncle was not really expecting him.

He tried to be polite about the waffles but couldn't help himself and took an enormous mouthful. They were so warm, sweet, and delicious, he thought he might cry.

"You know that every part we play in the underground, no matter how small it seems, is significant," Tante Marie said.

"Yes, ma'am," Espen said.

"And every part helps the rest. The Resistance has gotten quite organized now. There's Milorg, the military branch, and Civorg, the civilian branch, which is responsible for newspapers and propaganda, and there's XU."

"XU?" Espen asked.

"Intelligence," she said.

"You mean, like, spying?"

"*Ja,*" she said. "Each part is important. No part can exist without the other."

Espen stopped chewing for a moment. *Spying!* That's what he would like to do. That would be it, exactly! "My friend and I have done quite a bit of spying already," he said.

"Are you brave enough to continue delivering newspapers?" Tante Marie asked.

Espen snorted. "A few little pages like these? You don't have to be so brave to do that!"

He felt the heat of her eyes on him. "These 'little' newspapers," she said, "are illegal. They tell the truth about the

Nazis. You are aware that anything that criticizes the Nazis is forbidden? Just to *read* a different point of view than their own—they can arrest you for that! Not to scare you or anything," she added offhandedly. "Now, what do you say?"

Espen nodded. "I can do it."

The griddle steamed, and Tante Marie plucked a waffle out of it. She glanced at the newspaper again. "They've abolished the oath of silence of the clergy," she said. "The Nazis can demand the names of church members who oppose the Occupation or the names of Jews who have converted to Christianity. And if the clergy refuses? Imprisonment! What do they want with that list, do you suppose? Why do they need to know who the anti-Nazis are? Who the Jews are?"

It wasn't hard to get Tante Marie going, Espen thought. If she stayed distracted long enough, he could nab another waffle without her noticing.

"Those Nazis are like a troll with many heads." Tante Marie whapped more batter onto the griddle. "And those heads need to be chopped off"—she slammed the lid down—"one at a time."

"I assume you mean that as a . . ." Espen tried to remember the word they had learned in literature class. "Metaphor," he said.

"Sometimes a metaphor is the truest thing there is," Tante Marie said.

She continued talking, and Espen tried to listen, but he

couldn't think about anything except waffles and, when the ones on his plate were finished, more waffles.

". . . but a clever boy," she was saying, "can outwit them."

Espen slid his hand across the table toward the platter. "I'm not clever at all," he said. "You know, the other boys say I'm so foolish, I forget to pull my head in before I shut the window."

She turned and lightly slapped his hand with the back of her spatula.

"See?" he said. "I can't even steal a waffle without you noticing."

"Well, you can't expect to outwit *me*," she said. "But a troll is a different matter."

He watched as she picked up the entire plate of waffles, placed it in a pail, and covered it with a cloth. She was still talking. She had moved on to Norse mythology, and he tried to pay attention, but all he could think about was what the fate of all that deliciousness was going to be.

". . . you know the one I'm talking about," she was saying. "Not the Odin Swensen who works in the hardware store—I'm talking about Odin, the Norse god, the all-seeing god. But being all-seeing wasn't good enough for him, was it? He also wanted to be all-wise. So he went to see Mimir, who was the keeper of the Well of Wisdom."

Espen wished he'd been paying attention, so he'd know why she was talking about this.

Tante Marie continued with her story. "Odin said to Mimir, 'I want to know what you know.'

"And Mimir said, 'OK, but it will cost you.'

"'Fine,' Odin said. 'What will it cost?'

"'Your left eye,' said Mimir.

"Without hesitation, Odin plucked out his left eye and threw it into the well.

"'Now, tell me how to be as all-wise as you are,' Odin said.

"'The answer,' Mimir said, '*is to watch with both eyes!*'"

Tante Marie winked at Espen, then handed him the pail full of waffles. "Now, take this out to the barn." She shooed him toward the door.

"You're feeding these to the foxes?" he squeaked.

"It is possible to know too much," Tante Marie said. "Didn't I just tell you that?"

Espen walked to the barn slowly, wondering if Tante Marie was a little nutty. He didn't remember her warning him about knowing too much. He wondered how many waffles he could eat before he got to the barn. And did foxes even eat waffles? Didn't they eat mice and rabbits and things like that? Espen slipped his hand under the cloth and pulled out a still-warm waffle. Would the foxes pounce on him when he entered? What if they bit? And since when did foxes need a barn?

He took a bite of waffle and stepped cautiously into the darkness of the barn. It was so quiet, he stopped chewing.

Then the silence was broken by the whisper-soft sound of rustling straw and a startling, raspy cough that sounded not at all like one a fox would make. He swallowed his bite of waffle, which felt as dry as a wad of cotton. Then he set the pail down and slipped out quickly, before his eyes had a chance to adjust to the dark.

Espen could coast home. It was all downhill. He wasn't carrying anything incriminating, not even the jelly. He'd left it with Tante Marie in exchange for some eggs. *Mor* would be so pleased. He would have to make up a story about how he came by them and about what had happened to the jelly, which she probably wouldn't believe anyway.

He should have been able to relax, but he was trembling so much that his teeth were chattering, and not because he was cold. He was excited. He stopped and switched off his bike light. The moon had emerged from behind the jagged ridge; it was as bright and all-seeing as Odin's single eye, and it lit up the mountains, making them seem as big and fierce as frost giants.

What was going on in those mountains tonight? Espen wondered. He knew there were men and even boys hiding there. They had evaded capture or had escaped from Nazi prisons or were working for the Resistance from mountain huts. In the next valley over perhaps there was another boy, riding his bicycle along another lonely road. Up in the mountains a girl might be skiing a snowy trail. In the big city, boys walked down cobbled streets, delivering newspapers, many of them. On bicycles or skis, on foot, in rowboats, stopping by lonely farms, town houses, apartment buildings, and in sleepy fishing villages—all over Norway people were planning and plotting and doing. Now he was one of them. He had joined the Resistance. Soon, Tante Marie had said, he would have an assignment. And he had a code name: Odin.

The Commandant's Underwear

The house was dark. Espen slipped off his pack and his jacket quietly. He carried the eggs into the kitchen and made a little nest for them out of his wool scarf. His mother would find the offering first thing in the morning; he hoped it would make her smile.

Upstairs, all was dark, except a sliver of light from under Ingrid's door.

He quietly turned the knob and opened the door—and was greeted by a flying pillow. Espen caught it just as it was about to slam into his face.

"Hey!" he said. He shoved his glasses up on his nose and noticed Ingrid sliding something under the covers. "Now that you've turned ten, *Mor* lets you stay up to the wee hours?"

Ingrid held a finger to her lips.

"What are you doing up so late?" he asked.

"Nothing," she said. "Writing."

"I don't know what you're writing in that diary of yours," he said, "but be careful what you say. They're searching houses now, too, you know."

Her smile left her. "I know."

"And anything criticizing the Nazis is punishable, you know. *Seriously* punishable."

"I know."

He hadn't meant to scold her, and now she was frowning. But he had an idea. He slipped the pillowcase off the pillow, folded the pillow over his head and slid the case back over it. "My pillow hat," he proclaimed. "Do you like it?"

She laughed. "You are very talented at looking goofy." Then she added, more seriously, "Where have you been? I had to make up a story to tell *Mor* about where you were. I told her you went to a party after soccer practice."

"Thanks for that," he said. "Let's see . . . where have I been . . . ? I've been out on a very dangerous mission." He nodded his head, which made his pillow hat wobble.

Ingrid rolled her eyes. "I'll bet," she said.

"Yes," Espen sighed, leaning up against the door frame as he imagined a sophisticated spy might. "I, along with a few of my comrades, who shall remain unnamed, sneaked, under cover of darkness, into Gestapo headquarters."

"Oh, really?" Ingrid raised an eyebrow.

"Yes, indeed," Espen said, trying to look both nonchalant and serious at the same time. "Right under the noses of the guards, who were fast asleep and snoring so loudly, you could probably hear them from here." He held up a finger, and Ingrid cocked her head, listening.

Sure enough, a loud, rumbling snore could be heard through the walls.

"That's *Far,*" Ingrid said. Their father always snored.

"Oh. Perhaps you're right," Espen said. "It's hard to hear with this thing on my head."

"So, what were you doing there?" Ingrid asked. "At Gestapo headquarters."

"I was . . . stealing the commandant's underwear!"

"Is that so?" Ingrid said. "Let's see them."

"I don't have them—"

"I didn't think so."

"—because they're hoisted on the flagpole in front of the post office!"

Ingrid let out a guffaw.

"It wasn't so easy a mission as I let on," Espen said.

"Oh?"

"Because the guards woke up just after I'd grabbed the underdrawers. And . . ." Espen crept closer to her bed, his arms out and his fingers wiggling. ". . . I had to tickle them into submission!"

"Oh, no, you don't!" She pulled the pillow off his head and whacked him with it.

Still, he managed to get in some serious tickling.

The sonorous tones of their father's voice could be heard through the wall.

"Shh! Shh!" Espen said. He got hold of one kicking leg

and tickled the bottom of her bare foot. "Quiet! Look what you've done. You woke *Far*."

"Stop it! Stop it!" Ingrid screamed.

"Espen, stop tickling Ingrid." Their father's voice was loud and clear.

"Ha-ha. Caught red-handed!" Ingrid laughed.

Espen let up, handed back her diary, which had fallen to the floor, and put his fingers to his lips. "Now look what you've done!" he said. "You woke up the whole household."

He went to the door, then turned back. "Say," he said, "did you hear that Pastor Tronstad was asked if he would bury a German?"

Ingrid shook her head.

"He's a little hard of hearing, you know, and he said, 'What? A German? Sure, I'd be glad to bury *all* of them.'" Espen went out, laughing. He tiptoed to his room and flopped down onto his bed with all his clothes on. There were so many things to think about, but he was so tired. He thought for a moment about the big game coming up, and then, just before he dropped off to sleep, he wondered what Ingrid was writing in her diary. He hoped, for all their sakes, that it wasn't anything that could get her into trouble.

Ingrid's Diary

J*oke: What's the difference between the Nazis and a bucket of manure? Answer: The bucket*, Ingrid wrote in her diary. She would remember to tell Espen that one next time.

Everybody thought the Germans would be gone by now. But they're not. Why did they invade us? We were a peaceful country, minding our own business. And when will they ever leave?

Ingrid fumed, thinking about how the Germans walked into and out of the town's banks and shops and cafés as if they owned them, or stomped into peoples' homes and took things that didn't belong to them: blankets and food and even soap! The only soap their family had was a few slivers that *Mor* had hidden behind some books in the bookcase.

They act like they own the whole country! And they eat up the food that should be ours.

Just thinking about it made Ingrid's stomach complain. Dinner had been a thin stew of rutabagas and turnips and just the tiniest bit of pork.

They are as fat as pigs, she wrote. *Every time I see them,*

I want to kick them in the shins. I can't, so I kick them with my pen! Ha!

School was back in session now, after having been closed from the invasion, on April 9, through August. Ingrid had hoped that things would feel normal again once classes resumed. But even at school things were different. Some teachers who'd joined the fighting had been killed or captured during the intense battles in the weeks following the invasion. Even some of the older boys were gone.

Ingrid chewed her pen for a moment. Then there was Espen. It was nice that he'd come in to talk to her tonight, but she knew he had made up a story because he'd had to tell her *some*thing.

Now everybody has a secret, she wrote in her diary. *Maybe it's a secret stash of chocolate, an illegal newspaper, or a diary. Espen has a secret, too.*

What was it that had kept him out so late at night? she wondered. And why wouldn't he tell her? They'd never kept secrets from each other before.

Whatever his secret was, she intended to find out.

Waiting for the ferry

n the day of the big soccer match with the Tyssedal Tigers, Espen joined some of his teammates as they waited for the ferry that would take them down the fjord to Tyssedal. Stein, Per, and the twins, Leif and Ole, sat on a low stone wall, eating ice cream out of little paper cups. They stared at the street where columns of German soldiers marched in formation, something they did often. Frequently, like today, the soldiers were accompanied by a brass band.

"Ice cream!" Espen said, when he joined them. "Where'd you get that?"

The boys pointed their little wooden spoons at the small group of officers milling about across the street.

"You accepted ice cream from them?"

"'Accepted'?" Ole said. "No! We nipped these when their backs were turned. Go over there. Maybe you can swipe some, too."

Espen looked at the off-duty officers clustered outside the café. They were talking with some young women. "*Nei*," he said. "I'd rather starve."

The boys sat in sullen silence for a while, watching the

27

soldiers march in lockstep, swinging their legs high into the air in front of them.

"Why do they march like that?" Leif asked.

"Maybe they can't bend their knees!" his brother said.

"Maybe they haven't got any?" Espen said. "Just wooden sticks for legs?"

"I know what they haven't got any of," Per said.

They all laughed.

"Hey, don't laugh," Leif warned.

"They can shoot you for that," Ole added.

"Did you see the latest poster?" Leif said. "It says, 'Every civilian caught with weapon in hand will be SHOT . . . Anyone destroying constructions serving the traffic and military blah-blah-blah will be SHOT . . . Anyone using weapons contrary to international law will be SHOT.'"

"*Ja,* I saw that," Espen said. "On the bottom of the poster someone had written, 'Anyone who has not already been shot will be SHOT.'"

They laughed, and Espen did, too, sort of, but it made him feel sick. All these soldiers everywhere, always with guns, their metal helmets, the tramping of their boots—walking in and out of the stores, up and down the streets . . .

"Kjell!" he heard one of the boys call out, and he turned around to see Kjell striding toward them.

"Kjell!" Espen said. "Great! Move over, you louts."

Everyone shoved over so Kjell could sit down.

Espen smiled. He was younger than them all, and it had

been Kjell who had suggested him when the team had been short of players, and it was Kjell who had always stood up for him against his older—and bigger—teammates. Espen was happy Kjell had decided to play today. It would be just like old times. Later, when they were alone, Espen could ask him why he had been in that car full of Germans.

Now the soldiers were singing, ". . . *fahren wir gegen Engeland.*"

"What are they saying?" Ole asked.

His brother whacked the back of his head. "I knew you weren't paying attention in German class."

"They're singing, 'We're on our way to England,'" Espen said.

"I guess the war is over now," Per said, "at least for us."

"We tried to join the military, Ole and me, back when they were still fighting," Leif mumbled, his mouth full of ice cream.

"But we were too young," Ole said.

"And still are," said Leif.

"You can still join up, you know," Kjell said brightly.

The other boys turned and stared at him.

Kjell pointed to the soldiers in the street.

"Join up . . . with *them?*" Leif asked.

"Why not? They're here to help us," Kjell said.

"Help us how?" Stein said.

"They've come to protect us from the British, and especially from the Bolsheviks."

Leif snorted, spitting out his ice cream.

"We can protect ourselves!" Stein exclaimed. "We don't need Germany coming in and taking over our country!"

"Protect ourselves?" Kjell said. "The Norwegian military didn't last two months against the Wehrmacht! How well do you think we'd do against the Russians? Do you want those Bolsheviks coming and taking over our country? What if they invaded Norway, just like they did Finland? Germany can protect us from them."

"You're crazy," Stein told him.

"No," Kjell said, "you are. You have your head in the sand."

"You have your head up your—"

"Hey, look," Espen said, standing up.

Kjell interrupted him. "Germany is our friend."

"If Germany is our friend, why did they drop bombs on us?" Leif asked.

"They wouldn't have had to if we had followed our government's orders."

"The Quisling puppet show?" Stein said. "Is that what you're calling 'our government'? King Haakon rejected the Nazi demands. He said we should fight! He said we should resist!"

"The king is a traitor!" Kjell said.

"Take that back!" Stein jumped up and grabbed Kjell's coat collar, but Kjell knocked his hand away, stood up, and pushed him.

"The king ran away," Kjell said. He started to turn, but Stein caught him by the arm and punched him in the face.

Blood gushed from Kjell's nose, and Espen groped in his pocket for a handkerchief. Someone handed Kjell a paper napkin, which he held to his nose as he stalked away.

Espen went after him. "Kjell!" he called. "Are you all right?"

"I'm fine," Kjell said. "It's just a bloody nose." He turned and kept walking, so Espen had to jog to keep up.

"Why do you say things like that? Do you *want* to get into a fight? I mean, you don't really feel like that, do you?" Espen said. "You don't really believe the Germans are here to help us. With all their rules and arresting people and everything."

"We might have to give up a little bit of freedom, but it will be worth it to be safe." Kjell stopped and faced Espen. "Maybe you don't see it that way yet, but you will. Think about it."

Espen took a deep breath and said, "I saw you in that car full of Germans."

"When was that?" Kjell said.

"You know when," Espen said. "You saw me, too."

"Don't remember it."

"On the road to Fossen a couple of days ago. I was on my bike."

"Where were you going?" Kjell asked.

"To see my uncle," Espen answered. "Where were *you* going?"

"I don't recall I was even there," Kjell said. He turned and began walking away.

Could it have been someone else in that car? Had Espen been mistaken? It had been twilight, and the people in the car were more like shapes and shadows than anything else. Perhaps it had been someone who looked like Kjell, and Espen was being suspicious of his friend for no good reason.

But he felt a little sick to his stomach. Maybe because he was hungry. But maybe it was because he was pretty sure that Kjell, whom he had always considered his best friend, had lied to him. Even more unsettling was that he had lied so coolly, so casually. Espen wondered how many times he might have lied before.

"Kjell!" Espen yelled after him. "Aren't you coming to the game?"

Espen watched Kjell's back as his friend moved down the street. He knew there were plenty of Norwegians who were sympathetic to the Nazis. Vidkun Quisling, who was now head of the government, had welcomed the Germans. But, still . . . his best friend? He felt queasy and wanted to sit down. It was as if the whole world had shifted and was spinning wrong. Too fast. Too fast the wrong way.

Why had Kjell denied he'd been in that car full of Germans? Espen knew he was lying. But Espen took only a few more steps before realizing that he, too, had lied. He'd told

Kjell he had been going to visit his uncle, which wasn't true at all.

Flaming, devilish hell, he thought. *If nothing else ruins our friendship, lying will certainly kill it.*

He walked slowly back to the others.

"Is he coming?" Leif asked.

Espen shook his head.

"Now look what you did!" Per said to Stein. "You lost us our best player!"

"What do you mean?" Ole said. "What about . . ." He tossed his hair and held his nose high in the air. "*Aksel?*"

The other boys groaned, and Per aimed a spoonful of ice cream at Ole. The ice cream catapulted out of the spoon but sailed right past its intended target and continued toward the street. They all followed its trajectory. At first it looked as if it would hit one of the many helmets parading by, but at the last second, an officer stepped in front of it, and the ice cream landed with a splat on the back of his neck. He stopped.

Per took off running. The other boys stayed but turned their heads away, as if they had always been innocently focused on the other end of the street. Only Espen stared at the officer, curious to see what he would do. The German reached behind his neck and felt the ice cream. Then he turned and fixed his gaze on Espen.

The man could have been one of his own countrymen: strong and hardy looking, with fair hair and blue eyes, like a lot of Norwegians. He looked like someone who could take you on in a ski race. Maybe they *could* be friends, Espen thought, the Norwegians and the Germans. They were a lot alike, he supposed. At least, that's what the Germans kept telling them, anyway.

The officer smiled and nodded in a friendly way. That's what they all did. They all tried to act friendly.

But before the smile appeared, there had been a moment, a look. It was as if the officer had seen right through Espen. As if he knew about the comments he and his friends had just made; as if he knew about the dinner conversations around his family's table; as if he knew that Espen and his sister had a competition going for the best stupid-Nazi joke; as if he knew that, right now, there was a stack of illegal newspapers sitting on Espen's living room floor. It was the look you gave a dog when you knew he had chewed up your best pair of shoes and you intended to punish him. *I am the master,* it said, *and you are the dog.*

Perhaps it was a look meant to throw cold water onto his fervor, but instead, it was like throwing gasoline on a fire. The officer turned away, and Espen smoldered. He felt as if he was made of tinder and kindling, and all it had taken was this officer's eyes on him to ignite it.

The Soccer Game

Off we go to Tyssedal," Ole said as the ferry chugged down the fjord toward the little village.

"To play against the Tyssedal Tigers," Per said. "They're big."

"And tough," Leif said.

"And mean," added Ole.

The other boys on the team murmured agreement.

"You boys are babies," Aksel said, sniffing. He stalked to the other side of the ferry, where he stood facing into the wind, letting it blow his hair back. Espen thought he looked like one of the blond, blue-eyed Nordic lads the Nazis put on their posters.

As the ferry approached the village, the boys grew quiet, contemplating both the challenge of the opposing team and their playing field. The only place flat enough to play soccer in Tyssedal was a rocky ledge on the side of the mountain, high above the village. The boys silently slipped on their soccer jerseys, which were all so raggedy that even their team name, the Hornets, was barely visible anymore. But nobody had enough money to buy a new one.

The team disembarked from the ferry and began the long walk up to the soccer field.

The Tigers were already there; the Hornets could hear them shouting taunts down at them.

"OK, team, we need to concentrate," Stein said. "We have a shot at the championship; I guess we all know that. We also know that the Tigers are tough. So let's play our best—for ourselves, our coach and in the name of the king!"

"*Leve Kongen!*" the team cheered. "Long live the king!" All of them joined in except Aksel, who, as usual, walked separately from them.

They reached the field and began warming up, and Espen thought about how he and Kjell used to play together. They'd run up and down the soccer field until the sun slipped behind the mountains and their steamy breath hung in the frosty air. Finally, Espen—it would always be Espen—would get so tired, he'd lean over, his hands on his knees, gasping. "We have to quit!" he'd said once, and Kjell had replied, "Never! Press on until there is nothing left in you but the will to press on." Espen knew he meant it.

After the coin toss, Aksel began ordering all the boys into positions, even though Stein was the captain. The team had agreed that Stein would take over for their coach, who had gotten away to England to join the Allied forces. At least, that's what they'd been told.

Aksel finished by saying, "Ole and Per, you play midfield.

Leif and Stein, you can play defense, and you"—he pointed at Espen—"be goalie. It won't matter that you're in the net, because I'll keep all the action on the other side of the field."

Before the Hornets could protest, the referee blew the whistle, and the Tigers kicked off.

The ball went back and forth, but the Tigers were big and strong, and it was hard to play against them. The field was a frightening place to play. So high up on the mountain, any stray kick to their west would send the ball soaring out over the cliff and hundreds of feet down before it crashed into the salty fjord.

Espen stayed by the goal, and while the play was centered on the other half of the field, his eyes strayed to the black water below. He thought about the newspapers on his living room floor. One of the stories in the paper was about some saboteurs who had blown up a power station in Alvik. Maybe he would get an assignment like that! He imagined himself laying dynamite and tiptoeing backward, letting the fuse snake out . . .

Someone shouted, and he turned his attention back to the game. *Too late!* A big Tyssedal boy was charging toward him, taking a shot before Espen could even focus. The ball flew into the net, and the Tigers began to celebrate. Cowbells clanged in response from the village below.

Aksel stormed toward him. "You are as dumb as a bag of rocks!"

"It was too fast for me," Espen said.

"Keep your eyes open next time." Aksel shot him a dark look, then began admonishing the team to "pass the ball to me more. I'll score us some goals."

The Hornets kicked off, and Stein passed the ball to Aksel in front of the goal. Now it was just Aksel against the Tigers' goalie. He dribbled toward the net and took a shot, but the kick was much too forceful. The ball soared over the net and disappeared over the edge of the cliff.

Neither team had an extra soccer ball, so the match would have to stop while someone went to retrieve the lost ball.

Aksel pointed to Espen. "You're the goalie. You haven't been running. You go get it."

"I didn't kick it," Espen began to say, but he knew it wasn't worth arguing over. Aksel never listened to anyone.

Espen sprinted down the mountain to a fisherman's dock and borrowed a dinghy and rowed out into the fjord to recover the soccer ball. Mountains rose out of the water on all sides, a thousand feet high. Waterfalls thundered off the cliffs into the dark and endlessly deep fjord.

He saw the ball bobbing in the water and rowed to it, then leaned over the side of the boat to snag it. He didn't really want to look past his reflection on the surface, because he and Kjell had once seen a *draug* in this fjord. Or what they had decided must have been one. A *draug* could shift shapes. It could appear as a man or as a white horse, but this one had been a huge gray monster with a great dragon's head festooned with fleshy whiskers. He still saw it sometimes when he closed his eyes, or sometimes in his dreams.

So he kept his eyes averted as he reached for the ball, and he almost had his hand on it when he noticed that the water was wiggling. The fjord was teeming with jellyfish! Since he was familiar with the sting of jellyfish, he carefully used an oar to scoop the ball out of the water and into the boat.

Danger averted, he relaxed and rowed back to the dock. He tied up the boat and reached for the ball, but his hand shot back in pain. The ball was covered in stinging, poisonous jellyfish tentacles. How was he going to carry it up the mountain?

He could hear Aksel shouting at him. "Hurry up down there. We're all waiting for you!"

"Aksel doesn't have to carry a jellyfish-covered soccer ball," Espen grumbled. There was no other way to carry it, so he took off his jersey, wrapped it around the ball, and ran back up the mountain to the soccer field.

"Throw me the ball!" Aksel shouted several times, mixed with complaints about how long it had taken Espen to retrieve the ball.

Espen looked at Aksel. His face was flushed, as if he had been the one who had run down to the fjord and back. *Fine,*

Espen thought, *if he wants the ball so badly, he can have it.* He carefully unwrapped the ball and, without touching it with his bare skin, tossed it to Aksel.

"It took you long e—*Aaugh!*" Aksel screamed as his hands touched the ball.

The Intrusion

We won!" Espen hollered, flinging open the front door to his house. "We beat the Tigers, two to—" He stopped, dropping his rucksack at his feet.

A nicely dressed man stood just inside the entryway to the house. An agent for the Gestapo? Or a plainclothes Quisling policeman? Out of the corner of his eye, Espen caught a glimpse of a squat little local man he knew as the town laughingstock. He was practically prancing around their living room. His mother stood in the hall, a laundry basket resting on her hip. As the man touched one item after the next, her eyes stared red-hot daggers into his back.

The newspapers, Espen thought. His eyes strayed to the living room floor. Nothing there.

"*Mor?*" Espen said.

She glanced at him, the fire in her eyes melting into a mixture of relief and warning. "They're here for your scout uniform," she said. She shifted the clothes basket on her hip, and her eyes darted back to the pudgy little man. This was the fellow who made lewd comments to girls and kept company with the town drunks. Espen's friends had often teased him; the man was no doubt delighted at this opportunity to get back at Espen and his scouting friends.

"You look angry, madam," said the man at the door. "Please don't worry. We are not here to trouble you."

She turned to the policeman. Espen imagined he saw sparks flying from her eyes.

The man now turned to Espen. "You have been involved in Boy Scouts?" he said.

It was not really a question, Espen knew. Gestapo or Nazi policeman, it didn't matter: you didn't contradict these people.

He nodded.

The policeman glanced down at his clipboard and read, "You will turn in your shirt, trousers, cap, tie, and any badges you may have earned, whether they are attached to the uniform or not. All scouting activity is prohibited, any future outings are canceled, and scouts are not allowed to assemble in any way."

Espen went upstairs to retrieve his uniform, clenching his teeth against the bitter taste that rose in his throat.

Ingrid was standing in the hallway. "Espen," she whispered.

Espen mouthed the word, *Newspapers?* then nodded for her to follow him into his room.

"I don't know!" Ingrid whispered. "*Mor* made me come up here before she answered the door. What's going on?"

"Another stupid confiscation," he said, rummaging in his dresser drawers for his scout uniform. He glanced up at her pale face. "Don't worry. They're not collecting diaries. Not yet."

Espen delivered the uniform, the policeman deposited it in a bag, and the men gave obsequious little bows and backed out of the house. Espen turned to see his mother in the living room, wiping the furniture with a damp cloth.

"*Mor?*" he said.

"In the laundry basket," she told him.

Espen found the newspapers under the dirty clothes in the basket. "I'll get rid of these," he said, and he stuffed the remaining papers under his shirt and into his stockings.

"Take a ration card, and get some bread!" she said, as he went out.

At the Bakery

Espen left some of the papers on the bus, dropped several off at friends' houses, and had just a few left when he took his place at the end of the line outside the bakery. He wanted to stop thinking about what had happened at home. He wanted to think about the game.

We won! He mouthed the words, trying to retrieve the feeling of excitement he'd had after the game.

After a series of stupid moves in the early part of the match, they had pulled it together and beaten the Tigers, 2–1! Aksel and Stein had each scored a goal, and Espen had actually made some good saves after missing that first shot by the Tigers.

"Can you believe it?" Stein had said when the game was over and they were walking to the ferry. "We're on our way to the championship!"

Espen grinned.

"By the way, pretty good trick with the jellyfish ball," he said.

"It was kind of mean, I guess," Espen said.

"Anybody other than Aksel would have laughed," Stein said. "It would have been a good joke. You know he wasn't really hurt— it just 'stung' his pride a little."

Espen shrugged. "Maybe," he said.

"Aksel is the kind of fellow who will hold a grudge," Stein went on. "He'll try to get back at you. So what you did was either brave or stupid."

Espen laughed. "Probably stupid," he said.

The line moved ahead, and he was almost inside the bakery when he saw Kjell walking up the street. He had to tell him about the game! He bolted away from the line and raced up the hill.

Kjell turned and smiled at Espen, his light blue eyes twinkling in their usual amused manner.

Espen stopped, caught his breath, and said, "We won! If only you had been there! We're going to the championships! Isn't that great?"

"*Ja*," Kjell said. "That's great."

"You're going to play, right?" Espen asked.

"We'll see," Kjell said.

"We really need you!"

"I have other things to do."

Espen glanced at the package his friend was carrying under his arm.

"*Bestemor's* medicine," Kjell explained, patting it.

"Ah," Espen said. "How's your grandmother doing, then?"

"She'll be better once she gets this."

"It's the championship, Kjell!" Espen said.

"I said, 'We'll see.'"

Espen stared at him. He was suddenly acutely aware of the crinkling of the papers under his shirt.

"One thing . . . ," Kjell said. "It's about Aksel."

"What about him?" Espen asked.

Kjell moved closer to him. "I know you don't like him, but be careful. Don't cross him, Espen." His voice had lowered to a whisper and taken on an intensity that gave Espen goose bumps.

Espen rubbed the palm of his hand where the jellyfish had stung him.

"He . . ." Kjell hesitated. "He could make trouble for you . . . if he wanted to." He turned quickly and continued up the hill.

Espen headed back toward the bakery, his head swimming. Aksel could make trouble for him? What did that mean?

In the Café

AKSEL

From inside the café, Aksel watched as the scrawny goalie left the line outside the bakery and jogged up the hill to meet his friend. Although he couldn't hear what they said, he could tell they were happy to see each other.

He glanced down at his hands, at the red stripes still visible on his palms. If he thought about it, they still stung a little. That stupid kid and his stupid joke could go to the devil!

As he watched the two boys talking, Aksel replayed the game in his head. It had started out well enough, when nobody had challenged his right to give them their positions, even though he wasn't strictly the captain. He *should* be the captain! He would make a much better captain than Stein. What the team needed was discipline: someone to whip them into shape. They could be so much better if they had a stricter captain. It was mostly luck that they had won the game.

It was true, he had missed a couple of shots that he maybe should have had, but, really, it was the fault of the others on his team. None of them took the game seriously enough, the way he did. They were all jokers. And lazy, too. After the jellyfish episode, he had watched from the sidelines, furious at their lazy passes and the way they laughed and talked on the field. The game had been almost over before Stein had put Aksel back in.

When Aksel had run back onto the field, the other boys' smiles had faded. They played with him because they had to. Aksel knew they didn't like him. But he didn't care anymore. Because he knew something they didn't know.

Now he watched from the café window as the two boys parted and went their separate ways. He smiled. Soon, very soon, he knew that he would have a chance to get back at all of them, including that one walking slowly toward the bakery, who now had to take his place at the end of the line again. What a dunce he was—too stupid to keep his place, even, and too young to play on their team, anyway, that kid who had thrown him the jellyfish ball, the one whose name he had never bothered to learn.

ONE WEEK LATER

Soccer Practice

ESPEN

What good was a code name if you didn't ever get to use it? For the umpteenth day in a row, Espen had not heard a peep from anyone, hadn't been given any more newspapers to deliver or anything. He had kept himself busy by helping his father at the train station, but the anticipation was killing him.

"I wish I was doing something!" Espen blurted out, carrying an armload of packages and bundled letters into the mail car.

His father paused in his writing and looked at him over his glasses. "Aren't you doing something now? Turn that package this way, would you?"

Espen turned the package so the address faced his father. "Yes, but I mean, I wish I was doing something to fight the Nazis!"

"You should be a little more careful about what you say out loud," his father said. He scribbled something on his clipboard.

"Sorry," Espen said. "There just seem to be more and more of them every day! Look at all these packages they are

49

sending and receiving. Coming from Germany to somewhere in Norway. Going from Norway to somewhere in Germany."

He placed the parcels in the car, and his father, pen in hand, looked at each one and recorded something on his clipboard. What *was* he writing? Espen wondered.

———⧓⧓———

Espen was still wondering when he arrived at soccer practice. He sat on the sidelines, putting his soccer boots on slowly and carefully so that the tape that held them together wouldn't rip. Stein dashed up and said, breathlessly, "Remember Jotunheimen?"

"*Our* Jotunheimen?" Espen said. "*Ja.*"

"Meet up there tomorrow. Bring a hand saw."

A hand saw? Espen wondered. He glanced up, but Stein was gone, back on the field with the other boys.

Espen got out onto the field in time to hear Per say, ". . . they're going to be required to join the NS, the Norwegian Nazi party."

"Will they?" Leif said.

"Who?" Espen asked.

"The teachers," Ole told him. "Our teachers! They're supposed to sign a declaration of loyalty to the new regime."

The boys began to complain about all the new rules instituted by Quisling and his "NS," the Nasjonal Samling party. Like the stupid uniforms the NS had said they were going to require students to wear to school.

Espen practiced his dribbling techniques, bouncing the ball from his foot up to his knee and back down.

Leif said he had heard a rumor that there was going to be a Nazi sports association—mandatory, of course. "Nobody would join otherwise," he added.

"Ha-ha," Ole said. "Nobody will join, anyway. Just like the farmers and the fishermen haven't joined those Nazi organizations they were told to join, either."

"Like the whole merchant marine fleet didn't come back to Norway when the Nazis told them to," Gust said. "One thousand ships, now in the service of the Allies—take *that!*"

Espen wondered if the troll's heads that Tante Marie had been talking about had been a metaphor for all these new Nazi organizations everyone was supposed to join.

"Quisling and his Nasjonal Samling party really like to tell everybody what to do, don't they?" Leif said.

"And if you don't do it, they have the storm troopers from the group of Nazi thugs they call the *hird* come and beat you up," Ole said. "Did you hear about that boy in Oslo who got beaten up for tearing down a Nazi poster?"

Then Espen saw Aksel, sitting nearby, pulling on his soccer boots. His *new* soccer boots, Espen couldn't help but notice. How had he come by them? And how much of the conversation had he heard? Aksel seemed to be smiling smugly and glowering at the same time.

Then Leif said, "Hey, speaking of thugs, where's Aksel?"

Espen winced. The other boys, having by now noticed

Aksel sitting on the side of the field, were silent. Then Leif turned and saw him.

A car pulled up and stopped, and an official-looking man wearing a brown shirt and black tie emerged from it. He walked to the edge of the playing field where Aksel now stood.

"Brown shirt," Ole muttered. "That's a bad sign."

Next, three boys, also in *hird* uniforms, got out of the car.

"Young men!" the man called to the team. "This football club has been reorganized under the auspices of the Norwegian Sports Association. You'll be pleased to know that one of your teammates, Aksel Pedersen, will be your new captain."

Espen glanced at the other boys, all standing frozen in their positions.

"Athletes!" the officer continued. "It is now appropriate to cheer for your new captain."

The response was silence.

Finally, Aksel said, "Stein, you can stay on the team, playing defense. I'll put you into play when I can."

Stein walked to the edge of the field, picked up his jacket, and continued walking away without a word or a backward glance. Espen wondered what the other boys intended to do. Would they stay and be on a Nazi team? He knew they didn't want to, but there were those storm troopers . . . Who knew what kind of trouble his teammates might get into if they protested?

"Shall we play, gentlemen?" Aksel said. "We have a big game to prepare for."

Espen felt his heart pressing painfully against his ribs. He, along with all the other boys, wanted so badly to play for the championship. But to play as a Nazi team? Impossible!

Wouldn't the older boys do something? He was the youngest one. Surely he wouldn't have to be the first.

Looking at Aksel, so self-satisfied right now, believing he had finally won, Espen felt something like poison rush through his veins. He wanted to slug him and the storm troopers right in their smug faces. He felt his hands ball up into fists at his sides.

A taste, bitter as juniper berries, rose into his mouth as he thought of every humiliation he and his family had suffered lately: Watching that perverse little man snooping around their house. Having to turn in his scout uniform. How they all had to live in constant fear—even if you hadn't done anything wrong, you still had to worry that you might be doing something the Nazis wouldn't like. Wearing the wrong color, or not sitting next to a German soldier if there was an empty seat, or the million offenses they dreamt up while you were sleeping.

And now they'd taken over his soccer team! It was too much; it had to stop! Someone had to do something!

Jotunheimen

The bitter taste still lingered in Espen's mouth the next day when he hiked up to meet his friends at "Jotunheimen"—The Land of the Giants. It was just a huge flat rock they had discovered on a summer hike and had claimed as their own.

Ole flung himself down onto the rock. "Do the Nazis have to take over *everything*? We were *so close!* So close to playing for the championship!"

"We still can," Stein said.

"Oh, no," Leif said. "I'm not playing on any Nazi team."

"Me, neither," Espen agreed.

"No, of course not," Stein said. "But the game is still on."

The boys cocked their heads to look at him. Leif said, "Go on . . . ."

"Turns out the other teams wouldn't join the Association, either," said Stein. "Our opponents are looking for a field where we can play in secret. The game is still on!"

The boys whooped and threw their caps into the air. Per danced a jig.

Espen smiled. The Boy Scouts were meeting in secret, too, in a shop that made caskets, which was much more exciting than where they'd met before. They had to stagger their arrival times and go in the alleyway door so as to avoid suspicion. The Boy Scouts had gotten a lot more interesting all of a sudden. And attendance at meetings had dramatically improved.

"We're short players for the game, though," Per said.

"Maybe Kjell will play," Espen offered.

There was an uncomfortable silence.

Finally, Espen said, "I could ask him . . ."

"No," Stein said. "He's . . . we think he's 'striped.'"

The others mumbled their agreement.

"He'll come around," Espen said. "You'll see."

"No, he's changed," Leif said. "You'd better not mention any of this to him."

"And anyway," Ole said, "I know a couple of guys who'll be happy to play an illegal game of soccer."

"Enough of this banter," Stein said. "Follow me." Without a word of explanation, he struck off down the rock, across the trail, and toward the woods.

The others scrambled to their feet, grabbed their rucksacks, and followed.

"We can do more than play illegal soccer games," Stein said as he walked.

"*Ja!*" Ole said. "Let's kick some Nazi butt!"

Everyone laughed.

Then Leif said, "Do you mean, like saving Norway from the Nazis?"

Stein turned back to face the others, and said quietly, "That's exactly what I mean."

"The five of us?" Espen asked. "Against all two hundred thousand of them?"

"It might take a while. And I'm not saying it will be easy. Who's in?"

"Why not?" Ole said. "I can't think of anything I'd rather do."

"Sure," Leif said. "I'd like to get rid of the Germans more than anything on earth."

Per agreed.

The boys now turned to Espen. "Well?" Leif asked. "How about you?"

"Me?" Espen was a little surprised to be included. He was the youngest and, despite his good grades, somehow considered to be the dumbest. "Four-eyes," they called him, and also "numbskull" and "chowderhead."

But now they all turned to him expectantly.

"You were brave yesterday, Espen," Ole said. "The first to walk off the field after Stein."

Leif agreed. "I'm not sure I would have done it if you hadn't gone first. To tell the truth, I was a little scared of those storm troopers."

So was I! Espen thought. He had felt Aksel's eyes on him

as he left. He wouldn't be surprised if there were a couple of holes burned into the back of his jersey. "I was probably just too stupid to know better," he mumbled, pulling at a nearby weed and shredding the dried flower with his fingers.

"I doubt it," Stein said. "So . . . are you in?"

Of course he was in. He was in it already—although the other boys didn't know that. Ever since the Germans had invaded, Espen had felt as if the whole world had gotten off-kilter. Tipped wrong. If the world were flat, he could imagine things—soccer balls, shoes, whole houses, maybe—sliding toward the edge. The uneasy sense that at any moment they all might slide off the edge of the world into the darkness of space made him feel weak with fear or crazy with anger. He would do anything—anything!—to set the world right again.

"I'm in," he said.

"What are we going to do?" Leif asked.

"Let's blow up Gestapo headquarters!" Ole said.

"Do you know anything about explosives?" Stein asked.

"No."

"I thought not," Stein said.

"Even if we did know how, we can't do that," Per said. "The Nazis make reprisals for anything like that—they take random prisoners and execute them! What if they shot somebody because of something we did?"

"There are other things we can do," Stein said, "starting with . . ." He led them through a thick patch of woods and undergrowth into a small clearing. "Building ourselves a weapons depot."

"Whoa!" Ole said. "Really? Weapons? Where are we going to get those?"

"We'll see," Stein said. "For now, it can be a hideout. You all brought what I asked you to, right?"

Out of rucksacks came saws, a hammer, a hatchet, a rope, and a pailful of nails. The boys got right to work, clearing the area around a natural depression in the earth, dragging fallen trees into the clearing, sawing off the branches, and gathering moss.

Per sang,

> "I'm off to Oleanna
> I'm turning from my doorway,
> No chains for me, I'll say good-bye
> to slavery in Norway."

The other boys chimed in on the chorus.

> "Ole, Ole, Ole, oh! Oleanna!
> Ole Ole Ole, oh! Oleanna!"

As they worked, they took turns singing verses about a place where roasted piggies offered you ham sandwiches, beer flowed from springs in the ground, the cows milked themselves, and hens laid eggs ten times a day.

By the time their work for the day was done, the boys had a name for their hut: Oleanna. Espen wished like anything that Kjell could know about it. His friend would have loved to help build this secret place. When completed, it would have a heather-covered floor, log walls, and an earth roof. The whole thing would be camouflaged with moss and even a small tree or two planted on top.

Stein drew a big circle on the mossy ground. "This is the magic circle," he said, "and we are in this together. We keep each other's secrets, and the circle will protect us."

The boys stood inside the circle and placed their hands on top of one another's.

"We shall work tirelessly to save Norway from the Nazis," Stein said.

The others repeated it.

Espen felt that the day, which had seemed so gray, flat, and dull just a few hours earlier, had brightened. His friends looked strong and brave. *If anyone can do this, it will be us,* he thought. *And if we can't save all of Norway from the Nazis, maybe we can save this one corner of it.*

At the very least, Espen mused as he shouldered his pack for the hike home, *I can save Kjell.*

First Assignment

There would be moonlight but not too much, Espen thought, hiking up the hill with his skis on his shoulder. After a few kilometers, there was enough snow, and he stepped into his skis and slipped his hands into the straps of his poles.

The snow was good: newly fallen and soft. That was important, because it would be quiet. Now his skis whispered over it—"*shhh, shhh, shhh,*" they said—while Espen's heart could not seem to be quiet at all; it pounded away in his chest as if Thor himself were wielding it.

"Are you a good skier?" Tante Marie had asked before giving him this, his first real assignment as a courier.

"I ski well enough," Espen had answered.

"You know there is snow in the mountains," she'd said matter-of-factly. "So you will have to use your skis."

Espen nodded.

"It's not a difficult assignment," Tante Marie said. "It's only to retrieve something from a cabin."

"Where?" Espen asked.

"Hulringen," she said.

Espen had almost choked on his waffle.

"There's just one problem," Tante Marie continued.

Espen already knew what she was going to say: "The place is crawling with Germans."

Hulringen was a winter resort, and the whole area was known to be *Zutritt Verboten*, Access Forbidden. The Wehrmacht had taken over almost every available building. The ski lodge, the nearby farms—even family cabins and huts— had been requisitioned. But not the lonely little cabin where a revolver had been left behind and now must be retrieved.

Espen could hardly help feeling as if he was being watched. Not by deer or moose or fox, as he'd sometimes felt when he skied through the forest. This time, the eyes he felt on him were German.

He shouldn't be so worried, he told himself; they were terrible skiers. Some of them may have tried Alpine skiing in Germany, which involved shussing downhill and then being carried uphill by a lift. But most didn't have experience with Nordic skiing: trekking long distances over all kinds of terrain, up and down. He and his schoolmates had often laughed at the German soldiers learning to ski. There was a small hill near the school where they practiced. It was such an easy slope that even the kindergartners could manage it. It had been the scene of many wild episodes of one-ski races and jumping contests when they were younger. Kjell had won everything, as he usually did.

Now, schoolchildren would line up outside the school and laugh as the soldiers tumbled and tried to pick themselves up—often only to fall again—or have their skis carry them sideways or backward down the hill. Watching them trying to go uphill was even more comical. Even Kjell had laughed when a plump young soldier trying to herringbone up a hill ended up sliding down backwards, flailing the whole way.

Why weren't he and Kjell doing this together? Kjell should be on this mission. He would have been able to out-ski anyone. Kjell was the brave one; he would have been in the lead, and Espen would be much less scared at this moment. It probably would even be fun!

The cabin was just as Tante Marie had described it to him. Espen stepped out of his skis and went inside. Right away, he wished he was back outside and on his skis. He felt as if the walls of the cabin were a trap—a wooden box—and he was the rabbit. All it would take was for someone to pull the string and the box would collapse, and he would be trapped inside.

"Just stay focused," he told himself out loud, and he went to retrieve the revolver. It was where Tante Marie had said it would be, under a loose floorboard beneath the bunk.

So this is what a Colt .32 feels like, he thought. *Heavy. Solid. Dangerous.* He checked to see that it was unloaded, as he had been shown how to do, then stuffed it into his jacket pocket. After glancing out the window to make sure it was safe, he went out, slipped on his skis, and pushed off.

The moon had risen above the far peaks, and in the white moonlight everything—a rock, a stump, a distant tree—looked like a German soldier. Espen's heart whizzed, thumped, rattled, and banged around in his chest. He was jumpy, and his skiing was clumsy. At least it was downhill, he thought. But the farther down the mountain he went, the patchier the snow became until, finally, in the valley, it dwindled to nothing. Well, he thought, he was through the worst of it.

He stopped to take off his skis and walked the rest of the way into town. He would have to hide the gun at his house and take it to the fox farm the next day. So he hurried through the dark streets, ready to be home and safely in bed.

It was stupid, he knew, but he found himself walking right past Kjell's house. He burned with the desire to tell Kjell what he had done. What fun was it to do these things if you couldn't tell your best friend? If Kjell had been with him, then right now they would be crowing about how they had sneaked a gun out from under the Germans' noses—it would be as thrilling as stealing troll gold.

His steps slowed as he approached Kjell's house.

What would he say if Kjell came out right now? He shoved his hands into his pockets and curled his fingers around the revolver. If Kjell knew what he had done, he couldn't help but be impressed. Maybe he would want to join up with Espen and his friends.

Should he knock?

He glanced at Kjell's bedroom window. It was dark, of course—the blackout shades were pulled shut. Or perhaps nobody was home.

No. He knew he could not tell anyone what he'd done. Not his sister, not his friends, and least of all Kjell. This was not a game. He was really in it.

1942

IF THEY WON'T LEARN TO LOVE US,
THEY CAN AT LEAST LEARN TO FEAR US!

—JOSEPH GOEBBELS, NAZI GERMANY'S
MINISTER OF PROPAGANDA, REFERRING
TO THE NORWEGIANS

Ingrid's Diary

Before opening her brand-new diary for 1942, Ingrid paged through her diary from the previous year. So much had happened!

Almost every kind of food is rationed now, one of her entries read. *That is, if you can get it at all. Even potatoes are hard to come by for a lot of people.* Mor *dug up her flower gardens and planted potatoes instead. So we have potatoes and rutabagas and kohlrabi. Ish, ish, and ish. I am so sick of them all!*

Any books that the Nazis don't like (books that "damage national and social progress") are banned. Concerts, song lyrics—all censored. Dancing in public—now that's illegal, too. We aren't even allowed to celebrate our biggest holidays. May 1 and May 17 have been decreed "normal working days."

A few entries farther on she had written in big, bold letters, *GERMANY HAS ATTACKED RUSSIA!!!* Far *says, "Now Hitler has bitten off more than he can chew!" We can only hope.*

You'd think the teachers would ease up on us, what with all the hardships people are facing, but no. Not one bit of it. It's as if they are desperate to impart to us everything—everything they know, everything there is to know. Mor says they are "arming us with knowledge" before the Nazis take over the schools, which they are definitely trying to do.

There's a curfew now, and radios have been confiscated. If you are a member of the NS, then you can have your radio so you can listen to the propaganda stations. Some people have them, anyway, of course, hidden in clever places, even though the penalty is death. Death! For owning or listening to a radio. The same for possessing underground newspapers. Death!

A chill ran up Ingrid's spine. She had noticed Espen's skis leaning up against the house some mornings, still wet from melting snow, or his bicycle parked outside, spattered with mud. She knew he had been delivering newspapers, but she suspected that was not the only thing he'd been doing. He was not out *all night* delivering papers.

Sometimes he came into the house with his sweater damp and the smell of the mountains on him, his cheeks red from windburn.

"Don't ask," Ingrid's mother said, quietly laundering his mud-caked clothes, putting his filthy socks to soak in a tub in the basement. If *Ingrid* had come home with such dirty clothes, there would be some questions asked—she could be sure of *that!* But never a word was said to Espen.

What *was* he up to?

The Blank Page

Espen could hear the bell long before he reached the school. He had overslept—another late night. There had been a lot of them recently.

The janitor stopped him as he dashed into school and without a word handed him a piece of paper. So Espen came staggering into class, trying to struggle out of his jacket while still clutching the piece of paper in one hand.

"Place your essays on your desk . . . ," Mr. Henriksen was saying.

The strap of Espen's rucksack snagged on his jacket sleeve, so he set the paper on his desk in order to get himself untangled.

". . . and pass them forward," Mr. Henriksen went on.

Anna, the girl who sat in front of Espen, turned around and picked up the paper on his desk. "Is this your essay?" she asked.

Espen reached out for the paper.

"There's nothing on it at all!" She flipped it over, looked at both sides, then held the page out to Espen. But it was snatched up by a different hand, and the two of them looked up to see their teacher looking down at them.

"Please face forward and pay attention," Mr. Henriksen said, and he marched back to the front of the class, paper still in hand. "As I was saying . . . ," he began, but he stopped when the door to the classroom swung open and a Gestapo officer and two armed soldiers entered.

Espen watched as Mr. Henriksen's face went pale, and he saw his teacher's fingers curl tightly around the clean sheet of paper.

"Mr. Henriksen?" the officer said.

"Yes," the teacher answered. He stood ramrod straight and looked the officer in the eye, but Espen noticed the paper in his hands quiver; his hands were trembling.

"You are under arrest," the officer said.

The room had grown deathly still when the soldiers walked in. Now it was so still, it seemed that no one was even breathing—or *could* breathe.

Why? Espen imagined the students asking themselves. *Why are they arresting our teacher?* His gaze fell again on the paper. *Throw it away,* he willed Mr. Henriksen. *Throw the paper away.*

But Mr. Henriksen clung to the page as if it would save him.

"You will please come with us," the officer said, gesturing to the door.

Mr. Henriksen turned to the class and said in a steady voice, "Read chapters twelve and thirteen. You can have an extension on your essays until next week."

Then the soldiers took him by his arms and began to escort him out.

Although his knees felt as if they might buckle under him, Espen stood up at his desk. "Please," he said. "May I have my paper back?"

The officer snatched the crumpled page out of Mr. Henriksen's hands. "This is your essay?" He waved it at Espen.

Espen nodded slowly.

The officer held the paper out, and Espen walked with trembling legs to the front of the classroom.

"It is good to see you are so concerned with your academics," the officer said. Behind his thick lenses, his eyes were eerily huge.

Espen wished those lenses would somehow concentrate the sunlight coming through the window and cause the paper to catch fire.

The officer handed him the page with a terse smile, and Espen went back to his desk, sitting down in time to see the man absently rubbing his fingers together. The officer didn't seem to notice the white powder that drifted from his gloves to the floor.

The Encounter

spen walked to the train station with his head down. It was crazy. His teacher hadn't been arrested because he was involved with the Resistance. Instead, he and many others had been taken away just because they were teachers. Is that what Mr. Henriksen would call "irony"?

It was, at least, fortunate that Espen had gotten the paper back; being caught with it would only have made things worse for Mr. Henriksen. The message had probably been written in something simple, like baking soda. Any heat source would make the writing show up. The Gestapo would certainly know an easy trick like that. It was just lucky the officer had not noticed the white powder that rubbed off on his gloves.

Passing notes by tossing them into a wastebasket and relying on the janitor to distribute them to the right people had worked for a while, but it couldn't go on much longer. Espen supposed he didn't have to worry about it for now, anyway. School had been canceled.

He looked up to see Kjell coming toward him on the

street. He hadn't seen Kjell for months. Surely he couldn't still think of the Germans as friends! Kjell had always liked Mr. Henriksen. Espen would tell him what had happened, and that would make Kjell change his mind.

"*Hei,*" Espen said.

"*Hei,*" Kjell replied.

"You haven't been in school."

"No," Kjell said. "I'm going to the Rikshird school."

Involuntarily, Espen took a step backward. "The *hird* school?"

"You should join up," Kjell said.

"*Nei!*" The word shot out of his mouth so quickly, there was no way he could stop it. He should probably be more cautious, he realized, so he finished with, "My *mor* would never allow it."

A corner of Kjell's mouth twitched. "Your mama . . . ?" he said, a little sarcastically. Kjell had never been sarcastic before, and it made Espen feel unsettled, like being on a boat that suddenly pitched the wrong way.

"You should just get over your anger," Kjell said, "and join up. Anybody can see which way things are going."

Espen opened his mouth to speak, but Kjell went on. "If you get in now, you'll have your choice of jobs. If you wait, you'll have to serve, anyway. There's going to be compulsory service, and if you wait till then, you'll get the unpleasant assignments. It's worth it." He held up a box tied closed with string. Another package was tucked under his arm.

"What's that?" Espen asked.

"In the box?" Kjell said. "Cake! With *real* whipped cream! *Bestemor* is going to flip!"

Espen felt the hollowness of his own stomach, the huge emptiness of it. His breakfast of watery oatmeal was long gone.

"You should do it, Espen," Kjell went on. "You should join. Or else the Norway you know will be destroyed!"

"By the Germans," Espen said.

"No, by the Jews!"

"What?"

"All great cultures were created by the Germanic race, and of all the people in the world, we—the Nordic people— are the ones with the purest Germanic blood. Against us stand the Jews, who want to destroy us. If we don't win this war, Espen, it will be the end of the Germanic race, and the end of Norway as we know it."

"What are you talking about?" Espen said.

"We are living through *Ragnarok*, the time of reckoning. It's the final battle between good and evil, the Nordic blood versus the Jewish blood, and the Germanic blood must get the opportunity to build the new world."

For a few moments, Espen stood in bewildered silence. "I can't believe you . . . you really believe that! Where did you hear that rubbish?" he said. "Do you even know any Jewish people?"

"No," Kjell replied. "And I don't want to."

Espen thought he knew his old friend, but now it seemed that Kjell saw everything the opposite way he did. His great-grandmother would have said that Kjell had caught a troll splinter in his eye: night seems like day; day seems like night; everything right seems wrong; everything wrong seems right.

"You should think about joining," Kjell said. "I'll put in a good word for you with my superiors."

Kjell continued down the street. A neighborhood dog trotted alongside him, sniffing at the cake box and at the other package tucked under his arm. What was in *that* package? A ham? Bacon? Espen watched Kjell and his paper-wrapped package moving away. He imagined the trail of scent it left behind. And the stink that trailed from Kjell.

Espen felt the familiar empty feeling in his stomach. He was hungry all the time now, but he did not think the ham, the bacon, or even the cake would satisfy the consuming hunger in his belly.

Outside the train station, Espen watched a pair of soldiers march by. *Clong, clong, clong.* That was the sound their boot heels made when they struck the pavement.

He glowered at the soldiers—when their backs were turned—and went into the station. All he could think about was wanting to do something, *anything,* to get back at them for arresting the teachers, for clomping around with their iron-heeled boots, for twisting his best friend into someone he didn't recognize.

"Your father is in the mail room," one of the ticket clerks told him.

Espen hung up his jacket and took a load of packages into the mail room.

"I heard about what happened at school today," his father said, looking up from his writing. "It's a terrible thing."

"A lot of the teachers were arrested," Espen said. "What's going on?"

"Eleven hundred teachers from all over Norway were arrested. That's just to set an example. Many thousands more than that refused to join the Nazi's teachers' union and to indoctrinate their students with Nazi ideas. But they couldn't arrest them all, so they selected about ten percent of those who objected."

"What will happen to them?" Espen asked.

His father shook his head. "They are brave souls," he answered, "but they are not soldiers. They're not trained to stand up to the harsh treatment the Gestapo probably has in mind for them. Turn that box this way, would you?" he said, and continued writing.

Espen turned the box, its address illuminated suddenly by a shaft of sunlight. While his father's pen scratched against the paper, Espen watched the tiny glittering dust motes dancing in the light.

In a flash of insight as bright as the sunbeam, Espen realized that his father was recording addresses. Of course! The addresses of all the locations of German troops. Somehow, this information must be getting relayed to others . . . others in London, maybe?

Espen glanced at his father, who looked back at him over his glasses. A moment of understanding passed between them. Espen opened his mouth to speak, but just then his father was called into the office.

Espen stood still for a moment, wondering how many people were going about their work while also quietly undermining the occupying power in whatever way they could.

He sidled over to the office door and heard his father talking to another man.

"There's a risk, of course, but I don't think it's *that* dangerous," the man was saying. "Quisling would like to prevent the letters from being delivered, but—"

His father interrupted. "He's awfully young to be . . ."

But Espen couldn't hear the rest of it.

Were they talking about *him?* Espen wondered. He wasn't so young. Almost sixteen, after all. And there was something to be done? Something dangerous? He strode into the office.

"Who is awfully young, *Far?*" he asked.

"Have you been eavesdropping?" his father said.

"If you're looking for someone to . . . um . . . run an errand, I can do it," Espen said. "I want to do it."

"That's the spirit!" the man said, then turned back to Espen's father. "What did I tell you? He's just the ticket!"

The task was described to him, and the man finished with, "So, on Saturday, then? And, if any of those Germans come your way, just find a pretty girl to kiss!"

Espen felt his face flush. The only girl he wanted to kiss wouldn't be on the train—and, anyway, he'd never dare kiss her! Or any other girl, for that matter.

"If you have trouble, Espen," his father said, "it's always best to use the Gudbrandsdal Method."

"The simplest way . . . ," Espen began.

". . . is usually best," his father finished.

The Prisoners

INGRID

Sometimes Ingrid wondered why she bothered writing in her diary. She had once believed that words were powerful. A funny story made people laugh; a sad one made people cry. Words could inspire people to action. In fairy tales, at least, words could cast spells, enchantments. Stop trolls dead in their tracks. Save peoples' lives. Things like that.

But not her words. *Her* words didn't have that kind of power. One thing she knew for sure: her diary was never going to save anybody's life.

And what good would it do to write about what she had witnessed that day? How *could* she write about it?

She had been walking along the street, trying to get the white clouds of her breath to come out in neat rings the way Papa could with the smoke from his pipe. The fog was so thick, it was hard to tell what was her breath and what was fog. The rattling of wagons and clopping of horses' hooves made her look up and peer into the fog to see what would emerge. Horses came by, and wagons, and then, as if materializing out of mist, came . . . ghosts! Pale and bony as skeletons, with dark, sunken eyes. Then she noticed their ragged uniforms, and realized they were prisoners of war. Alongside them marched their German guards, wearing heavy wool coats and leather boots. One of the prisoners drifted near to her, snatched up a piece of turf, and stuffed it in his mouth. Others, she noticed with horror, were plucking horse manure off the street and eating it.

How hungry do you have to be to do that? she wondered. She had been hungry, but she had never been *that* hungry.

"And we thought we lived in a civilized country," a woman standing nearby said, shaking her head.

Ingrid had stood still for a moment after the procession went by. She did not think she could ever find words to describe what she had just seen. And, anyway, writing about it was not going to help those prisoners. She wanted to *do* something. Espen could do things. She could do things, too.

The "Thing"

AKSEL

ksel sat on the edge of his bed, rubbing his chin. Even before he stood up, he felt that *thing* working away inside of him like a worm inside an apple.

He got up and made his bed carefully, thinking about what was gnawing at him. He had an idea that somebody on the soccer team—maybe the whole wretched soccer team, or what had been the soccer team—was up to some kind of criminal activity. He suspected they had formed a gang or a Milorg group. If they had, he wanted to be the one to crack it.

He rubbed his chin again and thought he felt a bit of stubble. He could use a shave, he decided, and went into the bathroom. As he lathered his face, he tried to avoid looking in the mirror. There was a pimple right on the tip of his nose, and he did not want to look at it. He put the razor to his face without looking at his reflection, drawing it very carefully down the length of his jaw. How, he wondered, could he find out what the old soccer crowd was up to? It would help if he could get back in with them. He rinsed the shaving soap off the razor under the faucet and, without thinking, glanced in the mirror. *Ugh! That pimple!*

They didn't like him, though, and they never had. And now that he was an important member of the Stapo, the Norwegian secret police, and possibly soon to be promoted to the real Gestapo—he was on his way up!—he knew they liked him even less. He hadn't forgotten the day they had all walked off the field. There were a lot of things he hadn't forgotten.

There was no way he was going to be able to get anywhere close to them. Plus, he couldn't afford any wild-goose chases. His superiors were already displeased about the way he went off on his own to investigate things. He had been reprimanded about that before and reminded that he was supposed to *follow* orders, not *give* them.

What he needed was someone who had an in with the group, someone who—

"Ouch!" Aksel yelped. It was hard to shave without looking.

After stanching the blood on his chin, he continued shaving, now watching himself in the mirror as he did.

He tried to avoid looking at his nose, but the blasted pimple was like a beacon, drawing his eyes to it. Finally, he gave up, put down the razor, and went to work on the pimple, determined to squeeze it away.

He should find someone to help him. Someone who needed something, something that Aksel could provide. Food? A recommendation?

Or maybe . . . the pimple gave in with a satisfying *pop* . . . medicine.

Aksel held a damp washcloth to his nose. The pimple was bleeding now, too, along with the cut on his chin.

Medicine . . . yes, Aksel thought. In his opinion, it was stupid to try to save old people. Precious medicine supplies should be given to young, productive members of society, not people who were going to die soon enough as it was. But some people became very attached to their elderly relatives.

Aksel put a piece of sticking plaster onto the cut on his chin and one onto the tip of his nose and went down to breakfast.

"What happened to your nose?" his mother asked.

"Nothing." He reached for the newspaper and opened it. His mother placed a plate of bread and cheese in front of him. They even had a bit of margarine. Aksel hoped his mother appreciated that. Not very many people had margarine! It had taken a bit of maneuvering to get it, but he had done it. He knew how to do things. And he knew how to set a snare for his enemies. It might take a bit of time and a bit of maneuvering, but he could afford to be patient.

The Letter

ESPEN

As the train chugged through the countryside, Espen wished he were more brave. But since he wasn't, he would have to pretend to be. He practiced looking relaxed. He crossed his legs, then uncrossed them. He tried to fix his gaze on the snow-covered landscape but found his head turning back so he could keep an eye on the aisle, in case any officials came looking for travel permits. He didn't have one.

Espen glanced at his reflection in the window and practiced looking bored. He yawned, stretched his legs, and bumped the elderly lady sitting across from him. She gave him an amused look and went back to her knitting.

Next, he tried to look mysterious. Smart. Dashing. By what he could see of his reflection, he didn't think he was succeeding. If only he had a mustache! Maybe then . . .

He could have been on a ski holiday with his classmates. He looked out the window at the sparkling snow and the bright blue sky. Perfect skiing weather. His school chums would just now be tumbling out of their beds and pulling on their woolen knickers and sweaters, getting ready for a fine day of adventure in the mountains.

But, Espen reminded himself, he was doing something important: delivering a letter that was to be read aloud by nearly every clergyman in Norway to their congregations, a letter objecting to the violence of the *hird* and the tactics of the occupiers. He didn't know everything that was in the letter, but he knew that it criticized the Nazi regime, and he was only too aware of how the Nazis felt about any criticism whatsoever. Knowing that this criticism would happen in such a public way—on Easter Sunday morning, when the churches would be packed—gave Espen goose bumps.

The train slowed and pulled into the station at Fossen. Espen got up, slung on his rucksack, and, as soon as the train stopped, hopped out and trotted into the station. He'd have only a few moments before the train pulled out again.

Because of his father's position, Espen knew most of the station managers up and down the line and also many of the railway workers, and he had a pretty good idea of who was safe and who wasn't. He said a few words to the station manager, pulled an envelope out of his rucksack, and handed it to him.

The stationmaster nodded and placed the envelope in his inside jacket pocket. Espen sauntered, or tried to saunter, back to the train.

When he got onboard, he noticed an officer at the back of the car, so he stuffed his rucksack under his head and pretended to fall asleep. After he heard the man move past, he opened an eye. The old woman sitting across from him gave him a wink. She reminded him of his *bestemor,* with kind eyes and lots of soft wrinkles.

When the train pulled into the next station, Espen sat up and got ready to make another delivery. He shouldered his pack and strolled down the aisle to the exit. But when the door opened, his heart sank. Lining the platform were dozens of soldiers. Worse, a quick glance told him that they were searching bags. He hesitated. What could he do? Not leaving the car at this point would look really suspicious, but he couldn't be searched!

Then he heard a voice in his ear. "Give me your rucksack."

Espen turned to see the elderly lady who had been sitting across from him. He stalled for a moment, trying to decide what to do, and then remembered his father's advice. The simplest thing would be to give his bag to the woman.

She held out her hand, and he gave her the backpack.

He stepped aside to let her exit first. As she began to step down off the train, one of the soldiers moved forward to help her, and Espen watched in horror as the old woman handed the rucksack to the soldier.

The woman took the German's offered arm and struggled down from the train.

Espen was next, and he hustled by, hands in his pockets.

"No bag?" a soldier asked him as he walked by.

Espen turned back to him. "Just getting off to stretch my legs," he said. Out of the corner of his eye he saw the

German return his rucksack, unopened, to the old woman. The soldier even gave her a little bow.

Espen soon found the woman sitting on a bench inside the station, knitting. His rucksack sat at her feet. He sat down next to her, and she pushed it over to him with her foot.

"Everyone ignores them so much, they just love it when someone asks them for help," the old woman said. "My sister got the soldiers to carry her heavy suitcases full of black-market mutton all the way through the station at Oslo." She chuckled. "Now, run your errand, dear. The soldiers are all out on the platform, and if any of them come in, I'll distract them . . . And keep the 'look,'" she added.

"The 'look'?" Espen asked.

"What you were practicing on the train—looking stupid. That should work splendidly for you."

"Ah," Espen said wanly, and he went off to find a fellow he knew who was tagging luggage. When he found him, Espen slipped an envelope out of the pack and gave it to him. They exchanged a few casual words, and by the time he got back to the train, the soldiers had dispersed.

~~~⚬~~~

The next several stops went without incident. Espen spent some time wondering what he had done that had made him look stupid and how he might avoid it. But before he had come to any conclusion, he reached his destination. He got off, collected his skis from the baggage car, and boarded a bus for Follrud. From there, he went on skis to Riksdal. The last letter was one that he would deliver to the pastor himself.

His skis kicked up a fine, silvery spray of snow. The hum of the town and the buzz of the station faded away, and soon the only sound was the *chick-chock* of his poles and the whisper of his skis against the snow. He felt the tension and anxiety of the day evaporate with the steam that rose from his back, and he soon fell into an easy rhythm. He smiled and even laughed a little. It was a beautiful day for a ski—the snow winked and shimmered at him as if it were playing a part in the prank. Espen, the old lady on the train, and the snow.

"Outwitting the Germans once again!" he sang. He stopped to use his pole to draw *H7*, King Haakon's insignia, in the snow. He'd read in *Hvepsen,* one of the underground newspapers, that for every thousand Nazi posters, the illegal *H7* appeared ten thousand times. On roads, on rocks, on posters, and in the snow along ski trails. Maybe a million times by now.

"A million and one!" Espen said, and he skied on.

This might be the luckiest part of the whole trip, he thought. There was a girl from school who was on holiday with her parents at their family cabin near Riksdal. Maybe she would see him skiing alone—valiantly—across the mountain meadow and wonder: What was his errand that he looked so intent on his purpose? It must be something of grave importance that inspired him to move along with such strong and confident strides. Perhaps she would realize, just by his bearing, that he was—

His daydream was cut short when one of his ski poles accidentally planted itself between his skis, tripping him, and he fell face-first into the snow.

I hope she wasn't watching just then, he thought. He got up, wiped off his glasses, dug the snow out from under his collar, and brushed off his trousers. Just a few more kilometers to the Riksdal church.

Ingrid's Diary:
The Secret

The sounds of voices and the noise of clattering dishes drifted up from downstairs, and Ingrid knew she should hurry. But there was something she wanted to write about. A secret she couldn't tell anyone. Not anyone at all, except her diary.

I've done something, she wrote, *and I don't know if it's good or bad, right or wrong.*

"Ingrid?" her mother called. "You do remember that there's school today?"

I was waiting for Auntie Berit to finish work at the office where they handle the ration cards. When Auntie left the office, I sat for a while, staring at the boxes of cards sitting there, open.

First I thought: These boxes shouldn't be open like that, where anybody could steal them. I planned to mention it to Auntie when she returned.

But then I got started thinking about what I might do if I had some extra ration cards myself. I know it sounds bad! I know what you're thinking, Diary—if diaries can think, which I suppose they can't—so I suppose it's me who's thinking this. You are (or I am) thinking that this seems very wrong indeed. And as well as wrong, it seems bad.

But what if—

"You'll be late!" her mother shouted.

That is, I know it's wrong. But, on the other hand, maybe it is not so terribly wrong. I have stolen some ration cards! Ingrid scrawled, then slammed her diary shut and crammed it under her pillow. She jumped up and rummaged in her sock drawer for a few moments and pulled out a pair of stockings. Red. That would be a good color. The Germans hated it when you wore red. Red was a Communist color. That was what they said. But it was also one of the important colors of the Norwegian flag—a patriotic color.

"Ingrid," Espen hollered, "we're going to be late!"

Ingrid reached into the drawer again and felt around until her hand found a small bundle of cardboard cards. She stood still for a moment, looking at them. She couldn't just run downstairs with a fistful of ration cards! What would *Mor* say? Or Espen? They would want to know where she'd gotten them.

So Ingrid lifted her skirt, slid some of the cards into her underwear, and ran downstairs with her stockings in her hand. She sat down—carefully—on the bottom step to put them on.

Espen stood by the door, staring through the window at the street. "Can't you at least hurry up a *little?*"

What was he looking at? Ingrid wondered, and she craned her neck so she could see out the window. She could just make out a red hat bobbing above the fence. She looked at Espen. His eyes followed the hat.

Ingrid smiled as she tugged on her stockings. So, she thought, there *was* a girlfriend.

Her mother handed her a cheese sandwich wrapped in wax paper, and Espen tossed her a pair of snow pants.

"There's a ski contest today, remember?" he said.

She put on her snow pants and her jacket, and she and Espen headed out the door. But by the time they got out to the street, the red hat was just a tiny dot disappearing around a corner. Ingrid glanced at Espen and saw his face fall. Without a word, he collected their skis and poles and hoisted them onto his shoulder.

Ingrid was silent all the way to school, determined to find the girl in the red hat. But when she got to the school yard, it was a sea of red hats. Ingrid's friends Gretta, Astrid, and Solveig all had them on. Everyone was wearing one!

Red Hats

AKSEL

hat will it be next?" Aksel said. He folded his newspaper to the column and read aloud: "'Of course, one would be tempted to laugh if it weren't so tragic that the Norwegians are carrying on with this foolishness while the whole world is in upheaval.'"

"What kind of foolishness is that?" his mother asked.

"It's this *nisselue* business—these red stocking hats that everyone's wearing. It's so childish! It is just as Minister Lunde said right here in the paper, that the people who do these sorts of things make it seem as if we're living in an insane asylum! Wearing a paper clip on their clothing—what is that supposed to mean?"

"We bind together?"

"And matchsticks in their hatbands?"

"We're enlightened?" his mother said. Then she added quickly, "I would assume."

Aksel thought he saw a slight smile cross her lips. "Oh, and then there's the watch worn on the underside of the wrist. I forget what that's supposed to mean." He glanced at her. Her lips were pressed tightly together.

"I hope that you're not involved in harassing people for such minor offenses, Aksel," she said, "as I've heard those storm troopers—those Norwegian Nazis—have been doing all over the country."

"The *hird?*" Aksel snapped. "Where did you hear that?"

"Oh . . . ," she replied, "one hears things . . . You know."

"It's important to keep discipline, *Mor*," Aksel said. "People must not be allowed to laugh at their government."

"Really?" she said.

"The Norwegians must understand that the New Order is not to be made fun of! Norway has suffered from loose liberalism and permissiveness for too long. The Nazi party will reinstate order and authority. We have serious work to do, and we need the population to pull with us, not make fun of us!"

"Yes, I see," she said. "But Norwegians love their country just like anybody else, and you can't really blame them when they dislike another country for coming in and taking over. It's quite natural, really."

"Natural or not, it is also stupid what they do," Aksel said, "resisting in these childish ways."

One of her eyebrows went up.

"Don't look at me like that!" he said. "It *is* childish!"

"Perhaps so." His mother set one boiled egg on his plate and one on her own. "But it is also effective."

Aksel squawked in protest. "I can't believe I just heard you say that! After all I've done for you—I signed up for you,

you know—so you could have coffee and beef and butter and eggs, and even chocolate sometimes. I did it for you!"

She stared at her boiled egg as if it might crack open on its own. "For me?" she said. "Nice things and luxuries are not always the most important things, Aksel."

Aksel exhaled sharply and slammed the newspaper onto the table. "Even you!" he yelped, standing up abruptly. "Even you! Everyone is against me!"

He immediately felt guilty about his outburst. He shouldn't have spoken so severely. He knew that his mother suffered. Every day she grieved for his father, who had fought and died in the Winter War in Finland. How could the Norwegians forget that? His father, along with many other patriotic Norwegians, had gone to help the Finns fight against the Russians. Against Bolshevism! The same Bolsheviks the Germans were fighting against. How could the Norwegians not understand *that?*

But now, because of Aksel's decision, his mother's old friends avoided her. Most of their relatives did, too. The butcher sold her the worst cuts of beef; the baker gave her burnt bread. Some shopkeepers would ignore her so utterly that she couldn't even get served. But *he* could get food, and he brought her lots of things.

Like coffee, he thought. *Even if she has no friends anymore, she has coffee.* Because of him.

Still, he shouldn't scold his mother like that. "I'm sorry, *Mor,*" he said. "I know you've made a lot of sacrifices for me.

But I'm trying to make you proud. Today I am in charge of a ski contest. A meet at the school." He got up from the table, gave his mother a kiss, and went out, pausing by the hall mirror to adjust his tie.

He looked rather fine in his new uniform, he thought. Trim and fit and . . . well, handsome. He'd risen quickly in the ranks. He was quite sure there were any number of girls who were interested in him. He'd seen them glancing his way as he passed by on the street. He shouldn't wonder but that he could have his pick of them. It's just that he'd been too busy to have a girlfriend.

And why did the girl he liked have to wear a blasted red hat?

The Ski Contest

I
t was snowing when Ingrid and Espen lined up with the other students for the race. A fine day for a ski contest, even if it was a Nazi one, Ingrid thought.

The race was compulsory, of course.

"That's the way it is with Nazis," Kari said as they waited for the starting gun. "They want you to do something, so they make it compulsory."

"Compulsory uniforms," said Rosa.

"Compulsory propaganda hours for the NS," Arne said.

"A compulsory order to hang a portrait of Quisling in every classroom," Rolf added.

Ingrid joined in. "Compulsory visits to Hitler Youth exhibits!"

When the gun went off, they skied the first part of the course without hurrying. *In a leisurely fashion*, Ingrid decided she would write in her diary.

That was a good thing, because it was hard enough to ski with a bunch of cardboard stuffed into your underwear, much less to ski *fast!*

The skiers continued across a long field outside the

school together, talking and laughing, and then a message started being passed from one to another. By the time they had all reached the top of the hill overlooking the school grounds, everyone had heard the plan, and they all stopped, formed a long line, and turned back toward the teachers and Nazi officials waiting by the school. Then they began to sing the national anthem.

"*Ja, vi elsker dette landet,*" they sang—"Yes, we love this country"—all the way through to the end. They finished by shouting, "Long live the king!" and then they all turned and skied into the nearby forest.

It was a little bit crazy, Ingrid thought, but it sure felt grand! Once inside the shelter of the trees, the skiers slowed, stopped, and stood around laughing and chattering. Some decided to strike off for home or to town; others decided to go for a pleasure ski. No one intended to cross the finish line. Nor go back to school.

The skiers began to disperse and disappear into the fast-falling snow, laughing and calling out to one another, "Wait for me!"

Ingrid caught a glimpse of her brother, who was with a group of his friends, too. But he was looking at another, different group—a group of girls. Which one of them was he watching? Ingrid couldn't tell. She tried to move around to get a better view, but several skiers crossed her line of vision, and then her friends pulled on her arm.

"We're going downtown," they said. "Come with us!"

"I would," Ingrid said, "but I have something else I have to do."

Before she set off on her errand, Ingrid took one last glance at the group of girls and then at Espen, who was just then looking down, cleaning the snow off his glasses. But he'd clearly been gazing at one of them. Which one?

The Ski Contest

Espen listened distractedly to his friends while he kept one eye on Solveig, who was chatting with her friends.

Per skied up to Espen. "Did you get the message?" he asked.

Espen nodded.

"So, you're ready to go?"

"Uh-huh," he said. He could see Solveig over Per's shoulder. "Where am I supposed to go?"

"Stein says you should take this to Oleanna." Per handed Espen a rucksack.

Solveig had turned, and Espen could see her face now.

"SOE sent us a radio operator," Per said. "From England. We call him—"

Solveig looked up and caught Espen's gaze. Her cheeks were flushed and her eyes were bright from the cold. A shimmering scarf of snow draped her shoulders.

"—Snekker."

"What? When did that happen? Where was I?" Espen asked.

"Staring at pretty girls?" Per laughed.

Espen laughed and glanced at Per, who said, "Are you going to go or not?"

"*Ja.*" Espen slipped the rucksack over his shoulders.

"You have to go right away," Per urged. "Make sure nobody is following you. The Germans know there are radio transmissions coming from somewhere around there. So far they haven't found out where. Let's keep it that way."

"I'll be careful," Espen said.

Per skied off with the other boys, but Espen stayed behind, watching Solveig laughing with her friends, most of whom were now plunging down the hill toward town. She turned around and looked right at Espen, and then suddenly, somehow, the two of them were alone, surrounded by a curtain of falling snow.

Caught up in a sudden gust of air, the snow swirled and danced in sparkling ribbons around them. The other skiers had departed, their voices fading away; the whole world was blotted out, and there were only the two of them and this moment, a moment that might have lasted a minute, two minutes, hours, days, their whole lives, forever.

How long had he been standing there gazing at her, he wondered, as the snow drifted down, stopped, shifted, swirled, lifted, fell. And collected on his glasses.

I should say something, he thought. But no words came to him.

"Solveig!" her friends called from the bottom of the hill. "Are you coming?"

"We're going downtown," Solveig said. "Would you like to come along with us?"

Yes! he wanted to say. *Yes! I would!* But he felt the weight of the rucksack on his back—what was in that thing?—and he felt himself shaking his head, no.

Solveig turned, smiled back at Espen—and then she was gone.

Espen turned away and set off in the opposite direction.

The sense of falling snow stayed with him long after it had stopped, and for a while he skied along in a dreamy state. But then the air turned damp, and he suddenly felt chilled. He stopped to turn his collar up and realized how quiet it was, away from the rumble of army trucks, the stamping of boots on the pavement, the incessant "Heil Hitler" that was heard everywhere. It was so peaceful that all he heard was the sound of his own breathing, the soft thump of snow collapsing off a branch, the drumming of a far-off woodpecker. And a loud *snap*. What was that?

He stood absolutely still for a long moment. It was almost as if he could hear someone breathing. Or was he imagining things? It must be his own breathing he heard, he decided, and he continued on his way.

As he skied, his thoughts returned to the race and how everyone—all the students in the school—had sung the national anthem and shouted, "Long live the king!" There were too many of them to punish—because they had *all* participated. Like their teachers, who had won their battle against Quisling and the NS. Even after five hundred of those who were arrested were sent to a concentration camp, the remaining teachers still refused to sign on. Quisling had to give up and let the teachers go back to their—

Suddenly, his scalp prickled, and he stopped thinking about anything and just listened. Because now there really was someone. Right there, behind him.

The Joiner

urn around slowly," a voice said, in British-accented Norwegian. Someone from England. Per had told him a name. What was it? Why hadn't he paid attention?

He turned slowly. The first thing he noticed was the pistol aimed at his head. Behind the gun was a young man.

"Snekker!" Espen managed to sputter out. It made him laugh, a little nervously.

"What's so funny?" asked the man holding the gun.

"Well, it's kind of a funny name," Espen said.

"What's so funny about it?" The man dropped the hand with the gun, squinted, and let go a long fart. This made them both laugh.

"I just figured out your name," Espen said. "*Snekker* means 'joiner,' like a carpenter. You're the radio operator who 'joins' us with our contacts in England. I'm Odin."

"Brilliant boy," Snekker said. "Well, Odin, what did you bring me? I hope no more of that bread. What do they put in it, anyway?"

"They can't get decent flour anymore, so they lace it

with chalk. Or sawdust. Nobody really knows. Everybody calls it *fise brød,*" Espen said. "Fart bread."

"That's for sure," Snekker said. "That last loaf made me quite musical."

Espen opened the pack and pulled out two tins of sardines, a chunk of brown cheese, a pack of bouillon, a rutabaga, some potatoes, and a bunch of turnips. And a couple of dubious-looking loaves of bread.

"Is this really supposed to be edible?" Snekker turned the bread over in his hands, eyeing it skeptically.

"You could try waiting a week until it dries out. That's what a lot of people do," Espen told him. "By the way, do you know why the baker was arrested?"

"No. Why?" Snekker asked.

"Because he added flour to his bread dough."

"Good one," Snekker said. He glanced at his watch. "Well, it's just about time to wake up my sweetheart."

"Your sweetheart?" Espen asked.

"Everyone should have a sweetheart," Snekker said. "Haven't you got one back in town?"

"For all I know, she already has a boyfriend," Espen fretted.

"Maybe a German soldier," Snekker teased.

"No!" Espen said. "Anything but that."

"You never know, though," Snekker said. "I hear that a lot of girls like to go with the Germans. They give them silk stockings and chocolates and extra ration cards—romantic stuff, you know."

"Not Solveig!" Espen said. "She wears a *nisselue*."

"Ah, the red hat," Snekker said.

"Sometimes she pulls her collar through her button-hole," Espen offered.

"Sticking her tongue out at the Germans." Snekker laughed. "You've been observing her closely."

Yes, Espen supposed he had.

"Yet you haven't asked her out," Snekker said.

"I haven't even talked to her!"

Snekker laughed heartily. "Well, then," he said, "you have only yourself to blame. Hey, Odin, I have a joke, too. You know why there are no more eggs?"

"No, why?"

"Because in the country, the Germans get all the eggs, and in the city, they get all the chicks!"

Espen didn't laugh.

"OK, maybe that wasn't so funny," Snekker said. He looked at his watch. "Anyway, now it's time." He disappeared into the hut and returned with a very small radio.

"Oh, of course!" Espen said. "I've heard about these little British-made 'sweethearts.'"

"Go ahead," Snekker said. "Set it up."

After a few moments of crackling static, the radio fell silent. "I don't think it's working," Espen said.

"That can't be," Snekker replied. "It's almost time to transmit the information you brought me."

"I brought you information?"

Snekker removed a turnip from the bunch in Espen's rucksack and pulled a wedge out of it. From inside the turnip, he extracted a crumpled piece of paper. Then he fiddled with the radio himself. "Dead!" he said finally. "Do you know anyone who can fix it?"

"*Ja*," Espen answered. Ole had a job repairing radios for the Nazis, so they could listen to their propaganda stations. He also played a very useful role for nonlegal radio owners.

"We'll miss this transmission," Snekker said, "because you'll need to take this radio down to town and get it fixed or get a new part if you have to. Then you can bring it back up here."

"Why me?" Espen asked. "Why don't you—" But then he thought about Solveig going downtown, and maybe . . . "Fine," he said. "I'll take it."

"Make sure nobody sees you!" Snekker said. "If you go that way"—he pointed through the birch forest and down the mountain slope—"it's almost all good cover. There's only one open spot where it's marshland. Just don't be skiing through there when any Germans fly over."

"I guess the Germans know there are radio transmissions," Espen said. "They just haven't figured out where they're coming from."

"Well, if they come prowling about," Snekker said, "I've got a secret weapon."

"What's that?"

Snekker turned around, pointed his backside at Espen and let out a prolonged fart.

"I'll get some bread from Johansen's bakery when I'm in town," Espen told him. "They advertise that their bread goes 'two tones higher.'"

"Won't that be lovely?" Snekker said. "It'll be a regular symphony around here!"

Snekker's laughter followed Espen as he made his way through the stand of birches and on down the mountainside.

He sure makes a lot of noise for someone in hiding, Espen thought.

A few inches of powdery snow covered the icy crust underneath, making for easy skiing. Winding gradually down the hillside, he went from the birches to a stand of spruce trees and into a pine forest.

He tried to think of a good opening line in case he "ran into" Solveig. She would be downtown, and he would casually bump into her, and she would say, *Why, hello, Espen, here you are.* And then he would say—

What was that noise? He was suddenly aware that he had skied out into the middle of the open marshland Snekker had warned him about, and the noise he heard was the drone of an airplane.

By the sound of the engine, he could tell the pilot was flying low—it was a Fieseler Storch, a German spy plane. Espen glanced at his watch. Sure enough, it was exactly the time Snekker would have been transmitting radio signals. If he'd *had* a radio. But his radio—the very one these pilots were looking for—was in Espen's backpack, which suddenly felt very, very heavy.

Like a startled rabbit, he froze. He should not freeze, he thought, even as he stood there, frozen. They were sure to notice him there in the middle of the clearing, trying to look invisible. Nothing would make him look more guilty, unless it was skiing fast for cover. Which there wasn't any of, anyway.

Then he remembered the brave old lady who had handed his rucksack to the German soldier at the train station. *Be like that,* he thought. *Obvious and brave. Be so obvious that they don't believe you could possibly be trying to hide anything.* So, as the pilot flew overhead, Espen waved his arms, waved his ski poles, and shouted and smiled—like a kid who was excited to see an airplane fly so close and so low. So low, in fact, that he could see the startled face of the German pilot.

Good thing he can't see my heart jumping around in my chest, Espen thought, as the man in the cockpit waved back and steered the plane away.

He stood still for a few moments, listening to the receding drone of the plane, then set off again. The act of skiing steadied him, but it took a long time for his heart to resume its normal rate. Still, he knew he was getting smarter about all of this. *Smarter about seeming stupid,* he thought, and he laughed. Yes, and braver. Brave enough to face down an enemy airplane. But was he brave enough to talk to Solveig?

The Prison

Just outside of town, Espen caught a glimpse of red stockings rounding a corner. They were his sister's stockings. Where was she going? The only thing up that road was the German compound. What business could she possibly have there?

Espen ditched his skis in an alley and followed Ingrid, trying to be nonchalant, while his heart started up again, echoing loudly, as if inside an empty oil drum. He was afraid for her, walking so boldly, her schoolbag bouncing on her back, toward the camp. He was afraid for himself, too. He carried an illegal radio, and he was only too aware of the penalty he could face for that.

It was almost dark by the time Ingrid reached the edge of the compound. Espen, not far behind her, slipped into the cover of some spruce trees. Peeking out from the fringe of branches, he had a partial view of the camp. He could make out the barracks for the soldiers and the separate barracks for the prisoners of war. An armed patrol guarded the prisoners who hovered near the fence. Even from this distance, he could see how stooped and gaunt they were. He'd seen these POWs being worked like slaves, digging ditches and pushing wheelbarrows full of rock and rubble.

What was Ingrid up to? he wondered as she approached the barbed-wire fence. Soon the searchlights would start sweeping the area, illuminating everything in their paths. Did Ingrid realize that?

He caught his breath when a guard looked her way, and he lunged forward, ready to . . . do what, he didn't know. But Ingrid calmly reached into her bag and took out a package. What was she holding? And why had the guard, just then, turned his back? The prisoners acted as if they had been waiting for her, and they eagerly reached through the fence as she began placing what looked like small packages in their hands. Food. She was giving them food!

When it was all gone, she slung her schoolbag over her shoulder and walked away.

Espen retrieved his skis and hurried to catch up with his sister. A jumble of feelings coursed through him. He was angry at Ingrid for endangering herself. Yet he felt a little bit proud of her. After all, she was brave! She was also limping.

"That's pretty stupid, what you just did," Espen said once he caught up with her.

She turned to face him. "Have you been spying on me?" she asked.

"I just happened to see what you were doing back there. Where did that food come from?"

"Don't worry, there's still food at home . . . I stole some ration cards, if you must know."

Espen's jaw dropped. His sweet little sister had stolen ration cards? "Do *Mor* and *Far* know?" he asked. "I don't think they'd be happy to know you're doing such things."

"Why?"

"Because it's dangerous," Espen said.

"I'm not the only one in the family doing dangerous things," Ingrid replied.

Espen took her arm. "What are you talking about?"

"Well, what are *you* doing way out here? I know that you're not just delivering newspapers."

"You—you've been spying on me!" Espen sputtered.

"And *you* have been spying on *me*," Ingrid said, "so we're even." She limped away.

"What's the matter with your foot?" Espen asked. "Are you hurt?"

"No," Ingrid answered. "It's my shoe." She lifted her foot to reveal the sole of her shoe flopping. "I have to walk like this, or the sole flaps back and trips me."

Espen looked around. This was not the way he had intended to walk into town. This whole episode with Ingrid had gotten him sidetracked.

"Well, come on," he said with a sigh. "Mr. Levin's shop is just ahead. Let's get it fixed." The radio weighed heavily on his back. He wanted to get rid of it as soon as possible, but he had some money in his pocket, and he could pay for the repair of his sister's shoe.

"What if that guard had seen you, though?" he asked as he hurried her along.

"Oh, he saw me," Ingrid said. "I always go to that part of the fence, because of that guard."

"What do you mean, 'always'?" Espen said.

"I've been doing this for ages," Ingrid told him. "But *Mor* was starting to wonder where our food was going . . ."

"*Ja!*" Espen said. "Me, too! Listen, Ingrid, you could really get yourself into trouble!"

"They're not all terrible, you know, the soldiers. They're old men. Or just boys, not much older than you, Espen. They don't want to be here any more than we want them here. Do you ever think of that? I feel sorry for them. All the Norwegians are just as cold as ice to them. We won't talk to them; we won't sit next to them on a bus or a train; we won't answer them if they speak to us. Little kids won't even accept chocolate from them."

"It isn't any worse than the way we treat Norwegian collaborators," Espen said.

"I know," Ingrid replied. "The *Ice Front*—don't speak to them; don't have anything to do with them. That seems mean, too."

"The point is not to be mean. The point is to keep others from joining them. If people are 'on the fence,' perhaps they'll realize it's not worth losing contact with their friends and neighbors—or even relatives—just for a job or a radio or whatever reward they think they're going to get out of it."

They walked along in silence for a while. Espen thought of how Kjell and his grandmother must feel. They were getting "the ice treatment," too.

"Hey, did you hear we'll be having pork for Christmas?" Ingrid asked.

"Really?" Espen said. "How's that?"

"The *swine* will still be here!"

"Oh," Espen chuckled. "I get it. The German swine! Ha-ha!"

"That joke is sort of funny, but it sort of isn't," Ingrid said. "It's actually kind of sad. We will all have a poor Christmas, but the Germans will be even worse off than we are."

"How can you say that?" Espen said. "They're far more likely to have a pork roast than we are!"

"Yes, but what good is it if you're without your family?"

They arrived at the shop, and, relieved to at least be off the street, Espen pushed the door open. His glasses fogged up immediately, and he took them off and cleaned them with a corner of his shirt. When he put them back on, he froze.

Three smartly dressed men—secret police in plainclothes, Espen quickly surmised—were jotting things in notepads. One of them was going through the cash register drawer.

Espen started to back out, but Ingrid stepped forward.

"Yes?" one of the men said. The smell of his hair pomade made Espen's stomach turn.

"May I see Mr. Levin? I need my shoe repaired," Ingrid said. She held up her shoe for the man to see.

"The shop is closed." The man pointed to the sign on the door. The word OPEN faced the inside of the shop. Espen hadn't noticed it when they came in.

"But . . . ," Ingrid started to say.

Espen gripped her arm. "We'll get it fixed later," he said between his teeth. He pulled on her arm, but she wrenched free.

"Can we at least have a pair of shoelaces, so I can tie my shoe together?"

The man stared at Ingrid with his ice-blue eyes, then tossed her a pair of shoelaces from a jar on the counter. "No charge," he said. His eyes strayed over Espen's rucksack.

Espen pulled Ingrid outside and away from the shop.

"What was that all about?" she said. "Where was Mr. Levin?"

"We have to get out of here," Espen said. "Something smells bad." Like something very rotten being covered up by hair pomade, he thought.

A block down, Ingrid sat down on a step and said she wanted to tie the lace around her shoe.

"I'll be right back," Espen said. "Don't go anywhere."

He turned and walked back toward the shop, trying to

stay in the shadows of the buildings. Perhaps he could find out what was going on without being seen.

But, suddenly, Kjell appeared and pulled him into an alley. "What were you doing in that shop?" he hissed.

"Shopping for shoelaces," Espen replied. "They have very sturdy laces. Just a few pair left. If you want some, you'd better hurry."

"You shouldn't draw attention to yourself in such a way," Kjell said.

"I should draw attention to myself in some other way?" Espen asked. He tried to sound lighthearted, even though he was painfully aware of the contraband that he was, at that moment, carrying in his rucksack.

"It's not a joking matter, what I'm talking about."

Espen looked at him. Was this a threat? A warning? What was Kjell trying to say?

A couple approached from the other direction, and Kjell strode away. Espen stared after his former friend, then went back to Ingrid and told her to go straight home—no dilly-dallying—and to tell *Mor* to leave the window by the front door open as an all-clear sign, letting him know there were no unwanted "visitors" inside.

After the radio had been delivered for repair to Ole, Espen went home, took note of the open window, and went inside.

His father was sitting at the kitchen table, looking over some papers.

"What happened today, *Far?*" Espen asked him. "Ingrid and I stopped at Mr. Levin's shop, and—"

"Arrested!" his father exclaimed. "Because he is Jewish—arrested!"

"I didn't know he was Jewish," Espen said. "What will happen to him?"

His father shook his head. "I don't know."

"Didn't anyone know this was going to happen?" Espen asked. "Couldn't he have been warned, at least?"

His father crammed the dried berry leaves he now used as a tobacco substitute into his pipe. "Last night was the first anyone knew about it. Someone leaked the information to the Norwegian police. Our police chief called the few Jews in town and told them he was going to have to arrest them today. It was a warning, of course. But Mr. Levin didn't leave. Maybe because, like so many of us, he didn't believe it could really happen here."

"Just like we didn't think we would ever be involved in the war!" Espen said.

"We keep making the same mistake, don't we?" His father looked up at him.

"Why, though? On what grounds can they arrest a person just because he's Jewish?"

His father lit his pipe. "Hitler envisions a 'new Europe,'

a Europe of Aryan people only. Fair-haired, fair-skinned people—like us. He wants to hold up Norway as a model."

Espen's mouth suddenly filled with saliva; he went to the sink and spat. "We should have known," he said. "There were warning signs!"

"Yes," his father said simply.

~~#~~

Later, lying in his bed, Espen took off his glasses and put them on his nightstand. Without them, the room and everything in it was a blur.

He stared up at the ceiling. He had not been "watching with both eyes." He'd known that Jews had been singled out for harassment by the Nazis. He'd heard what Kjell had said about Jews, and he'd just listened in shocked silence. He could tell himself now that he had thought Kjell's awful comments were all stupid blather, that there wasn't really anything to it. But those ideas had come from somewhere. From someone who had power.

It made him feel helpless—like he often felt now, like how he'd felt when he watched Ingrid approaching the prison, and again when the guard had glanced her way.

But that had changed as he watched his little sister give food to the starving prisoners. In spite of all that had happened, somehow he felt as if this one small act of kindness could change everything. Shift the world slightly. Tilt the world a little bit back toward right.

ONE THING IS CERTAIN: HATE,
REVENGE, AND RETRIBUTION ARE NOT THE WAY.
THEY LEAD US BACK INTO THE ABYSS.

—FROM THE DIARY OF ODD NANSEN, NORWEGIAN ACTIVIST
IMPRISONED AT GRINI (NORWAY) AND SACHSENHAUSEN
(GERMANY) CONCENTRATION CAMPS

The Rabbit Plays Harmonica

nside the hut at Oleanna, Espen and his friends strained to listen to a tinny voice issuing from a small headset. The BBC news broadcast was nearly over, and they held their breath as several phrases were read: "The fox is dancing tango in the kitchen," then "Sleeping Beauty is asleep," and finally, "The rabbit plays harmonica."

"That's us!" Stein said.

They grabbed their packs and left the stuffy hut for the crisp mountain air. They stepped into their skis and snagged a couple of toboggans while Snekker came out to offer last-minute instructions. "Three fires in a line, a hundred meters apart!" he shouted after them as they began wending their way through the trees and up the mountainside.

"Espen," Per said as they skied side by side. "Do you ever feel as if someone is watching you?"

"Now, you mean?"

"No, just . . . sometimes."

"Have you seen anyone?" Espen asked.

Per shook his head. "It's just a feeling, I guess."

Espen was quiet. He had to admit that he'd felt it, too, at

times. A glimpse of someone disappearing around a corner. A face obscured by a newspaper. Just little things, probably meaningless. He pointed at Stein, Gust, Leif, and Ole, straggling along behind them. "I feel like we're being followed right now," he joked.

Per smiled half-heartedly, and they continued without speaking, their breath coming harder as the slope steepened. "Do you think we should worry about our tracks?" he said, glancing behind him at the black stitches their tracks seemed to make in the white snow.

Leif came up behind them. "Nah," he said. "The Germans never come up here. They mostly don't use skis. Besides, they never seem to notice anything like this."

It was true. Espen had often been surprised that the most obvious ski tracks were overlooked. Most of his friends would not only notice tracks, they could tell by a fox's prints if it had been hunting or just traveling. They could tell whether a grouse's wing marks on the snow had been made an hour before or were two days old. Yet the Germans didn't even seem to see the tracks a *man* left behind.

Even so, Espen had many times gone an hour out of his way to avoid leaving obvious tracks to a contact's house. Bicycling was best, but it wasn't always possible in the winter, and especially now that his bicycle was so worn out. Footprints and especially ski tracks had to be considered on the many trips he made. They were often long, lonely jobs, his courier treks. He enjoyed a job like this one, when he could work side by side with his old friends.

The group emerged into a meadow covered with a shiny crust of wind-polished snow.

"Let's hope the snow holds off for tonight," Stein said, nodding at the dark clouds clinging to the mountains.

The others began gathering firewood from among the trees, but Espen hesitated. Something had caught his eye, and he glanced across the clearing where the mountainside wore a vest of dark spruce trees. For a moment, something winked like diamonds or jewelry against the dark trees. Just the light catching something bright, probably. A patch of ice. Or perhaps the last rays of sunlight glancing off wet granite.

Espen joined the others with their task, hauling fallen branches out of the woods and dragging them into the meadow to heap on the bonfires that were being prepared. Luckily, the snow in the meadow had formed a firm crust, making their work easier.

When the fires were ready, it was still not dark enough to light them, and the moon had not yet risen. They would have to wait.

"Anyone for a scrimmage?" Ole asked as he removed his skis. He took a soccer ball out of his rucksack and kicked it high into the air.

Everyone laughed. "You realize you're going to have to carry that back along with everything else," Leif told him.

"*What?*" Ole said, "I carried it up. *You* can carry it back!"

Skis off, the boys began passing the ball to each other.

"What is everyone going to do about the Labor Service?" Leif asked, lobbing the ball to Per. "'All healthy Norwegians must register,' the NS says."

Per stopped the ball with his foot. "All the underground newspapers are urging men and boys to avoid registration at all cost," he said. "They say we'll be sent to fight at the Russian front, and younger boys will be sent to Germany."

"The only way to avoid it is if you already have a job that the NS thinks is essential," Gust said. He knocked the ball from under Per's foot and passed it to Ole.

"Like my job at the radio shop." Ole's kick to Leif overshot him. "The Nazis still need people who know how to fix their radios."

"And I've got my job at the fish . . ." Leif scrambled to catch up with the ball. ". . . factory. The Germans have to eat."

Stein reached the ball first, and sent it to Gust. "I'm all set," he said. Nobody worried about Stein. He was the one who took care of things for everyone else.

"Per and I are going to stay here in the mountains," Gust offered. "With the Boys in the Woods." He gave the ball a huge kick, sending it up and over the incline.

Everyone groaned, then climbed down the brushy hillside and thrashed around in the bushes until it grew too dark to see. Finally, Stein called them back to light the fires.

By the time the bonfires were burning bright, the moon

had risen above the mountains and was weaving in and out among the lacy black clouds.

Now the boys waited in tense silence. So many things could go wrong: The moon might disappear behind the clouds before the plane could get to them. Snow might move in, obscuring the drop zone, or the pilot might miss their signal fires. He might not be able to see the Morse signal or he might not be able to drop the load because of doors frozen shut or for any number of other reasons. Or, worst of all, it could turn out to be not a British plane but a "*Tante Ju*," a German transport chock-full of paratroopers.

Leif broke the nervous silence. "What are you going to do, Espen?" he asked. "About the Labor Service?"

Espen hesitated. He was almost seventeen and didn't have a job that counted. But he had become a valued courier for the Resistance. He had made countless trips all over the region and knew a lot of people involved in the underground. And they knew him. There was always the worry that his name—code name or real name—would be spoken to the wrong person eventually. He remembered now what Per had said about being followed, and about his own uneasy feelings. He wondered for a moment about the odd sparkle he'd noticed across the clearing earlier. He almost said something about it when a low rumble in the distance caught everyone's attention. As one, their heads turned toward the sound. Per got into position and began flashing the signal with his flashlight.

Suddenly, a big bomber roared overhead; its bomb bay doors swung open, and black specks plunged toward the ground, then, just as quickly, were swept upward as the parachutes opened. Dozens of containers drifted lazily toward earth, their parachutes glowing in the moonlight. They looked like jellyfish floating in the sea, Espen thought.

He and his friends stood smiling and waving to the brave pilot and crew who risked their lives to bring them supplies from across the ocean. For this brief moment, Espen felt connected to people all over the world, people who still lived in and fought for freedom. The weapons, radios, oatmeal, tinned meat, and chocolate that the packages contained were all needed and appreciated, but almost better was the feeling of being connected to the larger struggle, of not feeling alone and forgotten in the Norwegian mountains.

A few moments later, the engines revved to gain speed. With a thunderous roar that rocked the mountainsides, the plane sped away and disappeared. The friends got to work packing the supplies onto the toboggans and into their rucksacks.

"We'll take what we can to Oleanna," Stein said. "Some of this will go to the Milorg base farther up in the mountains. But we won't be able to get it all in one pass."

"Per and I can come back for whatever we can't carry tonight," Gust offered.

"You can walk in easily from the road down there." Stein pointed downhill, where they knew there was a small road that snaked along the mountainside. "There won't be any traffic along there at night. So, are we all set? Espen, did you decide what you're going to do about the labor draft?"

"I'm all right," Espen replied. "I can dodge the Labor Service people if they start looking for me, but I need a new bicycle. Mine is almost shot."

"Too bad! Wish I had known," Leif said. "I just bought a bike and sent it by train to a contact in Fossen. It's probably there already."

"I'll see if I can reroute it," Stein said. "Now, remember, boys, if anything goes wrong, head to Oleanna."

Just Before Dawn

AKSEL

A ksel pulled the car door shut behind him and rubbed his hands together. He turned to the two storm troopers in the backseat. "Shall we go catch ourselves some Milorg boys?" he said.

His protégés gave affirmative snorts.

"It's a foolish game they play, these bandits," Aksel said as the car got under way. "They really accomplish nothing, except to get people killed—often innocent people, if there is such a thing as an innocent person in all of Norway. These Milorg men, these XU agents, the Civorg people—they are like mosquitoes, jabbing their tiny, annoying, but not very dangerous stingers into the bare necks of the Germans. They think they are protecting Norway, but from what? From their real protectors!"

"There are only a few of them, really," Hans said from the backseat.

"Don't be stupid," said Lars. "There are more and more of them every day."

Aksel shot Lars a look.

There was no point wasting his wisdom on the two men in the backseat. *Men!* Aksel thought. That was a bit of an exaggeration! At twenty, he was older than either of these mouth-breathers. They were just bullies who saw a chance to do what they liked to do by joining the *hird*. They knew how to do one thing and one thing only. And they were good at it. So, at least, Aksel didn't have to damage his gloves or risk having blood spattered on his uniform. Still, he hoped to be rid of them soon. One more promotion and he'd be able to shake off these stupid boys and get to work with the professionals, the real Gestapo men.

"Turn off the lights," he said to the driver.

"Are you crazy?" the driver said. "On this winding road? It's still dark!"

"There's enough light to see."

"But not for someone to see us coming around the corner," the driver told him.

"Exactly," Aksel replied. "Now you're catching on."

The lights were switched off, and the car continued slowly up the mountain, carefully navigating the sharp curves. As they rounded one of the switchbacks, the driver slammed on the brakes. Some strange thing lay in the middle of the road. Something round and pale.

There was an uneasy silence in the car. After a moment, Lars whispered, "It looks like a head." Hans snickered nervously and then was silent.

"Wait here," Aksel said, and he got out of the car.

The predawn light cast an eerie blue glow on the coating of snow. Aksel approached the object in the road cautiously.

Then he laughed. It was only a soccer ball. He reached down to scoop it up but stopped. Were those voices he heard? He signaled the driver.

The driver threw on the headlights, sharply illuminating Aksel, the road ahead, and two young men who had appeared from around the bend and stood blinking in the twin beams.

"Well, well, well, if it isn't a midfielder and a forward— am I right? On your way to a soccer match?" Aksel said, holding up the ball. "Or perhaps"—he pointed to their heavy rucksacks—"coming from an airdrop?"

The car doors slammed as the two storm troopers stepped out onto the road. Maybe, Aksel mused, that promotion would come sooner than he thought.

The Bicycle

They'd gotten a name out of the soccer players—although not without some pain, Aksel reflected, as the car pulled up in front of the house in Lilleby. Well, that's what those Milorg bandits should expect. Even so, Hans and Lars had laid it on pretty thick. When one of them took off his boot and started beating the smaller of the two boys with it, that might have been more force than was necessary. But they *had* succeeded in getting a name—probably a code name—and also an address, and Aksel hadn't even gotten blood on his uniform.

"Draw your guns," Aksel said grimly as they quietly exited the car. "I'll go first."

He knocked on the door, and, a few moments later, it swung open. He recognized the fellow immediately: Stein, captain of the soccer team. In a glance, Aksel noticed the surprised look. Stein's hand was still on the doorknob, and there was a pile of papers on the floor behind him. There were hurried footsteps—someone was getting away, Aksel thought. He noticed Stein's subtle step back, the door beginning to shut . . .

Aksel's mind couldn't quite keep up with everything, and his finger, as if of its own accord, squeezed the trigger of his gun. The gun went off, and Aksel saw Stein go down, shot point-blank through the chest. He couldn't think about that right now, he told himself, moving past the fallen man and into the room. The retreating person was gone; the breeze pushed a lace curtain in through an open window. Aksel pulled the curtain aside and, in the early-morning light, noticed the dark outline of trees that lined the river below. He waved Lars and Hans around the side of the house to go after whoever had escaped while he turned his attention to the papers.

Aksel moved them away from the expanding pool of blood that was seeping from the dead man, whom he did not want to look at or even think about. He wished it had been someone he didn't know. Not that he'd ever liked Stein, he reminded himself. Still, he felt a little sick to his stomach, so he went into the kitchen to pour himself a glass of water.

Through the window he could see Hans and Lars walking back up the slope to the house. They were empty-handed. He pulled himself together and tried to think about practical considerations. He shouldn't have shot Stein without even questioning him. He was likely to be reprimanded. Unless . . . unless he could get more names, especially important names, or many names.

By the time the storm troopers came in, Aksel was back

in the front hall, going through the papers, every single one of them in code and signed with code names, no doubt. "Go through the pile," he said to the men. "See what you find."

"Here's something!" Hans plucked a luggage ticket out of the pile. "Something going by train from Lilleby to Fossen."

"Is there a name on it?"

"*Nei*," Hans said, tossing the ticket to the floor.

"Are you an idiot?" Aksel said. "Pick that up."

Hans picked up the ticket and handed it to Aksel.

"Put all these papers in something, and let's go," he said, heading for the door.

At the station in nearby Fossen, Aksel presented the ticket to the agent and received a bicycle. He gestured to Hans to take a look.

"Just a bicycle," Hans said. "So, big deal."

"That's where you're wrong," Aksel told him. "Look at this." He pointed to a stamp on the bicycle; it read HEGVIK'S SPORT SHOP. "Somebody bought this bicycle—wouldn't you agree?"

Hans nodded.

"And this little piece of paper"—Aksel held up the luggage ticket—"may be a way to track someone down. Isn't that obvious?"

Hans backed into a shadow.

"So . . . on to Hegvik's." Aksel smiled. "In Lilleby."

He enjoyed the chase. He enjoyed the unraveling of a mystery. He wished right now that he was accompanied by real Gestapo men instead of these stupid Norwegian punks. The Germans often acted as if they were naturally smarter and more quick-witted than the Norwegians. Aksel would have relished showing them that a Norwegian could be just as smart as they were. Smarter.

The drive from Fossen to Lilleby took longer than it normally would have; they had to stop twice for sheep on the road and another time to change a flat tire. By the time they reached the bicycle shop, Aksel had worked himself into a lather. He told the men to follow him in and bring the bicycle with them. As they stepped inside, the sole employee in the shop was heading into the restroom.

"This is why"—Aksel paused to spit on the shop floor—"the Norwegian economy is not working. The employees would rather take a piss than wait on a customer." He continued through the store to the repair shop in the back and spoke with a bike mechanic in a greasy apron.

"Who bought this bicycle?" Aksel demanded, gesturing at the bike.

The repair man wiped his hands on his apron and went

to the front of the store, where he dug around in a drawer for a long time before finally producing a receipt.

Aksel recognized the name: Leif Eversen. They had gone to school together, and, like Stein, they had played on the same soccer team. And Aksel knew where he worked: the fish factory.

Back in the car, Aksel began to think about Leif and the entire soccer team and how much he hated all of them. Leif had been one of those who had walked off the field the day that Aksel had been made captain. The thought of it brought a metallic taste, like gunmetal, to his mouth. He rolled the window down and spat. Well, he thought, it had been a worthless team, anyway. None of them were any good. And the young one—that kid who'd played goalie—he was as dumb as a post. Like that stupid employee at the bike—

Aksel had a sudden, jolting realization: That bike shop fellow had never come out of the bathroom the whole time they'd been there. "The devil!" he shouted. "That Hegvik's man! He wasn't going to the bathroom—he was climbing out the window! Step on it!" he screamed at the driver.

Aksel knew he was pushing it, acting like he had more authority than he really did. Shooting Stein had been a mistake and would probably get him into trouble. Maybe he could say it was self-defense, if the *hird* boys would keep their mouths shut on the subject.

If he could get Leif to talk, though, and turn up more names, *important* names, these transgressions might be overlooked. So he'd just better find Leif. And soon.

By the time they screeched to a halt in the factory yard and piled out of the car, Aksel had collected himself.

"This is how it's done, men," Aksel said, stopping for a moment to adjust his jacket. "Step by step. Wasting no time. Tighten the noose around the neck of your prey." He bent to brush the dust off his boots, noticed the blood spattered on them, and rubbed it off with his thumb.

He wanted to look his best when he arrested Leif. Or, if necessary, killed him.

"It's Full of Gestapo in There"

ESPEN

A s evening fell, Espen set out on his bicycle for Leif's house. The front tire was a little low, and the wheel rim was bent, but not so badly that he couldn't ride. The bike would at least get him as far as Leif's to drop off whatever was in the envelope he'd been given to deliver. It had rained earlier in the day, and he could see that it had snowed up in the mountains. It looked like it would soon snow here in the valley, too, but maybe not so much that he couldn't get to Leif's.

He thought about Ingrid's birthday the next day, her thirteenth. He should have gotten her some kind of gift. A cake, he thought, as he puffed up the hill, would have been nice.

He also had to think of a good joke, because she was winning their joke competition. He reviewed the one he had heard earlier that day so he could tell it to her: Responding to a loud knock on the door, a Norwegian asked fearfully, "Who is it?" "It is the Angel of Death," came the ominous reply. "What a relief!" responded the Norwegian. "I thought it was the Gestapo."

That was a good one, he thought, as he wheeled his bike

through the garden gate. Now, if he could just come up with a nice cake, with cream on it—even ersatz cream would be a treat.

He'd gone up the stairs and was just reaching for the door knocker when a loud hiss stopped him.

"Psst!"

Espen stopped. His hand fell away from the knocker.

"Don't go in there," the voice whispered.

Espen turned. "Kjell?"

"Go down the steps and back the way you came," Kjell said. "Nice and quiet."

Espen stared at him.

"Now!" Kjell said between clenched teeth.

Espen hesitated.

"It's full of Gestapo in there," Kjell said before disappearing between the houses and into the darkness of the backyards.

Espen had no reason to trust Kjell anymore. None at all. But he had to decide: Knock on the door and go inside, possibly into a trap? Or turn around and go out to the street, possibly into a trap? His throat tightened, but he knew he was going to trust Kjell. Maybe for no good reason.

Breathe, he told himself. He hopped down off the steps and pushed his bike toward the front gate. *All right,* he thought. *So far, so good. Just go on calmly.* It began to look as if he would make it to the street without being noticed, and he began to breathe again.

But just when he thought he was free and clear, a car screamed to a halt in front of the house, and three Gestapo officers emerged, then raced toward him, pistols drawn.

It had begun to snow, the flakes softly thumping all around him like a thousand tiny heartbeats. Out of the corner of his eye, Espen saw sheets on the neighbor's clothesline. It was too gentle a night for gunfire, too sweet-smelling. What if he died right here, right now? Without saying good-bye to anyone? His parents. Ingrid. Why hadn't he ever managed to work up the courage to talk to Solveig? If he lived, he would do it. He would not hesitate.

He was painfully, poignantly aware of the fresh scent of clean laundry and—abruptly—the perfumed shaving soap of the officers as they rushed past him.

. . . As they rushed right past him!

For a moment he felt as light as a feather, as if he were not standing but floating. Perhaps he had suddenly become invisible, because the officers ran up the stairs and into Leif's house without a glance in his direction.

Espen continued walking his bike past the Gestapo car. Then he noticed a second one, parked farther down the street. How had he not noticed it when he first arrived? He didn't know what made him do it, but he glanced inside as he passed by. There, on the backseat, was a box, a bakery box, tied with string. About the size of a cake.

The window was rolled down, and, feeling a little giddy, he reached in and snagged the box.

Somehow, Espen found himself seated on his bike. Somehow, his legs began to pedal. Slowly, as if he had not a care in the world, he steered his bicycle down the street. Slowly, the roar in his head subsided. Slowly, his stomach unclenched, and feeling returned to his limbs. The cool breeze ruffled his hair as he picked up speed, squeezing the tears from his eyes as he sped down, down, down the hill.

He was flying now, the cake box dangling from the handlebars, his mind racing in time to the whirring of the chain. *Go! Go! Go!* he thought. But go where? Leif would try to hold up under torture for as long as he could to give the others time to go underground. He was sure of that. Even so, he might reveal Espen's name, or, if he didn't, someone else might. Who knew how many people the Gestapo were in the process of finding and arresting? Espen knew a lot of people. He knew too much. Right now he knew one thing for sure: He couldn't go home.

Riding his bike through alleys and quiet side streets, Espen thought about what to do next. He couldn't go to any of his friends' houses. That was risky for him and for them. His bicycle chain ticked away, reminding him of the time passing. Curfew had come and gone, and he was still out on the street. Where could he go? Where could he go that would be safe?

An arc of car lights made him pull his bike behind a row of spruce trees. He listened to the purr of the auto's petrol engine: German. While the car slowly passed by, he peeked through the branches. The Gestapo car. He turned and looked through the backyards and could just see the rear of Solveig's house. Nobody, not even Ingrid, knew about his crush on Solveig. Even Solveig didn't know! But could he go to her house late at night and ask to stay there? It certainly wasn't what he had envisioned as a first date.

The car had turned and was slowly coming back toward him. *Move!* he thought. *Do it now!*

Espen pushed his bike through the yards and parked it in the shrubs behind Solveig's house. He stared up at the dark windows. Because of the blackout curtains, it was impossible to tell if any lights were on or not. It would be terribly rude to wake everyone. He walked in tight circles, trying to work up the courage to knock on the door. He laughed when he realized his heart was beating as hard as it had when the Gestapo had come racing at him at Leif's house. Hadn't he just vowed to talk to Solveig if he lived through that episode?

Quickly, before he lost his nerve, he put his hand to the door and knocked.

The Cake Box

A window on the second floor slid open, and a familiar face appeared. "Espen!"

It was Solveig. At least she hadn't called him "chowderhead," he noted. That was encouraging.

Moments later, he heard the side door being unlatched. "Hello!" she said, brightly, as if he was just coming to pay a casual visit. "What brings you by?"

Espen opened his mouth but found himself speechless. "I . . . uh . . . that is . . . ," he stammered.

Solveig grabbed him by the arm and pulled him inside. "Sit down," she said.

What could he say? He couldn't tell her everything. "I am . . . uh . . . I have to avoid the Labor Service," he blurted out.

Solveig's parents came down the stairs, her mother wrapping her robe around her. "Hello," she said. "Is there trouble?"

"You remember Espen," Solveig said. "Ingrid's brother? He has to stay out of sight for a while. The Labor Service is looking for him."

"Ah," her father said. "Well, you'd better stay here, then. You can sleep on the couch, close to the basement door. If you hear anybody knocking, take all your things and run down into the cellar right away. Be sure to take your shoes, too."

He led Espen down the stairs. "We can handle whoever might come," he said. "There's the storm door that takes you out the back, if necessary."

Espen tried the latch and saw it would open easily.

When they returned upstairs, Solveig's mother said, "You must be hungry. Let me see if I can find something for you to eat."

Espen remembered the cake box, and even though he'd meant it as a gift for Ingrid, he held it out to Mrs. Dahl. "Here's a little something," he said.

"My goodness!" she said. "That's very kind of you! What is it?"

He shrugged. "A surprise?" he said.

"You don't know what's in it?" Solveig laughed.

"Not really," Espen said. "Haven't you heard the joke about the lady who came out of a store carrying a paper bag, and all the others standing in line asked her what it was? 'I don't know,' she said, 'but it was only one *krone!*'"

The Dahls laughed at the joke, and Solveig said, "I'll fix some tea, Mama. You sit down."

Mr. and Mrs. Dahl sat at the kitchen table with Espen, and they talked while Solveig put a kettle on the stove and took out cups and saucers. Espen heard the pleasant rattle of teaspoons being placed on saucers, and then Solveig's sharp intake of breath when she opened the bakery box.

"Espen?" she said.

He got up, went to the counter, and looked into the box. There was no cake. He saw at a glance that the box was full of letters and documents, and that at least some of them were in code. And they seemed to be spattered with . . . yes, blood.

He shut the box quickly. It had been stupid of him not to look! He stole a glance at Solveig, and she signaled to him with her eyes: *Don't say anything to my parents.*

Espen replied with a small nod of agreement and set the box under his chair.

"Sorry!" he said. "My mistake. Nothing to eat." As he sat back down at the table, his limbs felt jellylike. What had he done? Now he had introduced dangerous papers into the Dahls' house, containing who knew what kind of secret information.

With great concentration, he returned to the conversation. "It has begun to snow," he said.

"Has it?" Mrs. Dahl said. "It's so hard to tell with these drapes shut."

They talked about goings-on about town and about the new compulsory labor law.

"I've heard that Hitler is conscripting men ages sixteen to sixty to defend Germany," Mr. Dahl said.

Espen told a joke about how Hitler was so desperate, he'd even conscripted Methuselah. "Yes, *that* Methuselah. Nine-hundred-year-old Methuselah from the Bible!"

Everyone laughed, and Espen thought how odd it was to be sitting in this kitchen telling a joke, as if life was going on as normal, when he knew that outside and all around him, things were spinning wildly out of control. He didn't know what might have happened to whoever had been the intended recipient of these papers. Didn't know what had happened to Leif and Ole or any of the others. He didn't know when and if he himself might be discovered. Didn't know whether if at his own home, right now, the Gestapo were waiting for him. Everything seemed very tenuous and uncertain. Yet here, around this kitchen table, in this small circle of light, he felt intensely alive. Was it because of the events of the evening or the dizzying proximity of Solveig, whose face shone as if in full sunlight? He was pretty sure he was falling in love, as crazy as that seemed. The thought almost made him laugh out loud.

They finished their tea and rose from the table, placing their dishes in the sink as if it had been just any evening, as if Espen had been a member of their family for years. Solveig brought him a down coverlet, and they all went off to their beds as if nothing unusual was happening outside these walls, as if things were not, as Espen knew they were, falling apart, or spinning out of control or, perhaps, sliding off the edge of the tilted earth.

Espen sat on the couch, listening to Solveig's soft footsteps retreating up the stairs. Then he opened the box and went through the papers.

They were all in code. He had often carried papers very much like these. Had they reached their destination? Had they already been deciphered by the wrong people? And whose blood was this?

He shoved the papers into his rucksack, burned the box in the fireplace, and sat on the edge of the couch, trying to puzzle everything out.

He should leave now, he thought, before he brought the Gestapo to Solveig's house. Or perhaps he should stay a little longer, to make sure the patrols were off the streets. He would just lie down for a few moments, he thought, and then he would go.

Oleanna

n the middle of the night, Espen woke. He couldn't say what had awoken him, but he had been dreaming of the *draug*. The enormous gray beast circled, swimming just under the surface of the water, opening and shutting its mouth as if trying to tell him something.

Espen opened his eyes to the darkness of the empty living room and sat up, suddenly remembering what Stein had said: "If anything goes wrong, go to Oleanna."

He got up, slid into his jacket, picked up his rucksack, and then slipped quietly out the side door. The snow had stopped, and in the predawn hours the town was bathed in a milky blue light. Espen thought about the strangeness of the whole night: the Gestapo, his bicycle ride through town, the dreamy sight of Solveig at the window, the warmth of the down cover that had sent him so immediately to sleep, the dream of Kjell warning him to . . . But that had not been a dream. Kjell had been there, at Leif's house, and had warned him about the Gestapo. Or *had* he dreamt that? The whole night seemed a mix of dreams and real-life nightmares.

At the edge of town, Espen stashed his bicycle and set off across snowy fields toward the forest. He paused for a moment. Should he worry about his tracks? If this was all a dream, did it matter? Was he dreaming still? he wondered, as the sun rose, turning everything a delicious, buttery yellow: the snow, the sky, and even the little hidden cabin . . . against which, glinting and gleaming in the morning sun, leaned three pairs of skis.

When next he blinked, Leif and Ole were emerging from the hideout.

Espen heaved a sigh. "You two are a sight for sore eyes," he said. "Are Per and Gust here, too?"

"No," Leif replied. "Apparently, they were picked up on the road to the airdrop."

"The word is, they were badly beaten," Ole added. "The Gestapo must have gotten something out of them. We don't know what—or how much."

"What happened?" Espen said.

Leif rubbed some wax onto the bottom of their skis while Ole explained his part of the story.

"All we know is what happened to us," he said. "It happened this way: Jens, who works at the bike shop and is a Milorg man, saw the Gestapo come in with a bicycle that he recognized as the one Leif had bought. Probably the one he intended you to have. So Jens slipped into the bathroom, out the window, and across the street to the radio shop to find me. I went straight to the factory to find Leif.

"I was just warning Leif when the Gestapo car drove up. The hooligans came toward the factory office, but the front man—honestly, I think it was Aksel Pedersen!—bent down to tie his shoe or something, and I went casually out the side door, and he didn't notice me. I went straight home, got our skis, and came here while Leif . . . well, he can continue the story," Ole finished.

"After Ole left," Leif said, "I climbed a ladder to the loft above the factory office and slipped into an air shaft. The thugs searched all over the whole factory. One of them even climbed up into the loft with a factory watchman as a hostage. 'What's that?' the Gestapo agent said, and the watchman answered, 'An air shaft.' Without even looking inside, the agent slammed the air shaft door shut, trapping me inside!

"I waited until I was sure they were gone, then shouted and hollered until the watchman found me. I didn't go home—I was sure the Gestapo would have headed there next. Instead, I came straight here," Leif finished.

"Now we're headed to Sweden," Ole said.

"Maybe you should come with us," Leif said. "You can use Snekker's skis and boots—"

"Hey!" Snekker came out, shouting and belching. "Who's—aw, it's *you?* Fine, then. Go ahead, take my skis. Someone will bring me another pair."

Who would that be? Espen wondered. "Maybe Stein?" he said.

"No one's heard from him," Leif said. "We're worried."

"Do you think the Gestapo has my name?" Espen asked.

"Not from us," Leif said.

"But until we find out everything that happened, we won't really know who they know about."

"And don't forget, there's the Labor Service, too," Ole added. "If the Gestapo doesn't get you, the Labor Service will."

Espen wondered what to do. It would be safest to go with Leif and Ole, of course. He could always return when things settled down.

But their group was fractured now, and *somebody* had to stay to put the pieces back together. And then there was Solveig . . . Finally, *finally,* he had spoken with her. And now he was going to *leave?* He thought of the circle of warm light around her family's kitchen table the previous night. He longed to sit there again, among those good people, with Solveig next to him, smiling. She had even laughed at his jokes!

And then there were the papers, weighing heavily on his back.

"Let me borrow your skis, Snekker," he said.

"You're coming with us, then?" Leif asked.

"No," Espen said. "Not yet."

A Shadow

spen squinted into the sun and watched until Leif and Ole had disappeared among the crisp, windswept waves of snow. Then he turned and skied west, with the sun on his back. Tante Marie would know what to do with the papers he was carrying.

Suddenly, he remembered the document he was supposed to have delivered to Leif.

He glanced back over his shoulder. Leif and Ole were gone. Espen knew he wouldn't be able to catch them now. He supposed he'd better take a look at the paper, so he pulled the envelope out of the secret pocket his mother had sewn into the inside of his jacket and opened it.

Darling, it began.

Hmm . . . that's odd, Espen thought.

I miss you so much. How I long for your sweet kisses and embrace.

What was this? Espen turned the paper over, but the other side was blank.

Why must we be so far apart? Soon we will be together, and I will be in your arms. We will—

Espen skimmed the rest of the letter, but it just went on and on in the same vein. He tried to discern anything of importance but found nothing.

Had he just risked his life to deliver a love letter to Leif? He resisted the urge to crumple the paper and throw it as far as he could. Instead, he shoved it into his pocket. If he ever caught up with Leif, he would wave this evidence in front of him before he . . . before he punched him in the face!

He skied on, angrily jabbing his poles into the snow. He would show Tante Marie the letter. He hoped she would be angry, too. He also hoped she would be making waffles.

She was not. She was shoveling snow off her roof when Espen skied into the yard of the fox farm.

"Tante Marie!" Espen called up to her. "What are you doing up there?"

"What does it look like I'm doing?" she said. "I'm shoveling."

"You shouldn't be up there!"

"It's very difficult to shovel snow off the roof from down there. You should try it!" She stopped and leaned on her shovel.

"I'll try from up there if you'll come down here," Espen said. "Let me do it."

"*Ja, ja,*" Tante Marie said.

Espen held the ladder while she climbed down, wheezing the whole way.

"Take it easy," he said. "No hurry." He helped her over

to a snowbank to sit down and said, "You shouldn't be doing things like that."

"I'll be all right," she puffed. "I just need a minute to catch my breath."

Espen climbed up the ladder and surveyed the situation on the roof. "You must have had quite a storm."

"*Ja.*" Tante Marie practically gasped the word. "It's a good thing you came to see me."

"So I could shovel the snow off your roof?" Espen asked.

"That was just a lucky thing," she said. "Actually, I have to tell you—" She stopped abruptly and waved one hand at him while holding the other to her chest.

Espen clattered down the ladder and knelt beside her. "Are you sure you're all right?" he asked.

"The truth is . . . " Tante Marie's face was ashen. ". . . I don't know how much longer I'll last. It's a race now to see who gets me first: the Gestapo or my bad heart."

Espen's own heart raced. *No!* he thought. *Not Tante Marie!* "We'd better get you to a hospital," he said.

"No," she said, waving his concern away. "It's not that bad. Let's go inside."

He helped her into the house, and she sat down at the kitchen table. When her breathing and color had returned to normal, she gestured to a stack of crispy flat bread and a block of brown goat cheese. Espen shaved off long curls of the sweet cheese to place on top of big squares of bread. He gave one to her and took one for himself.

"What did you have to tell me?" Espen asked.

"Why don't you tell me first why you came to see me," Tante Marie said.

"Something's gone wrong," he said between bites. He told her about Leif and Ole and about the box of blood-spattered documents. Per and Gust had been beaten up and, he supposed, arrested. He could feel his face getting hot with anger as he told her that in the midst of all this, he had risked his life to deliver a love letter to Leif.

Tante Marie held out her hand.

Espen gave her the crumpled letter. She glanced at it, then said, "Let's take this out to the barn."

In the barn, she motioned for him to move a bale of straw and then to lift the trapdoor underneath. From a hole in the floor he hoisted up a box. He opened the lid to find an assortment of small vials and bottles.

She held the letter up to the shaft of sunlight that streamed in through the window, turning it this way and that. She smoothed the paper and set it on the straw bale, then chose a vial from the assortment and dabbed some of the liquid on the page.

Espen watched in amazement as pale blue writing appeared between the dark black sentences of the letter.

"Invisible ink!" he gasped, then read the words aloud as they appeared: "*Your group has been compromised. Some-one has a shadow.*" He thought for a moment and then said, "A shadow?"

"A spy," Tante Marie said. "Someone in your group is being followed."

Espen and Tante Marie looked at each other. "Maybe you," she added.

"Me?" Espen whispered.

"Do you think there's an informer in your group?" Tante Marie asked.

Espen shook his head. "No. Not possible."

"Someone from outside, then," Tante Marie said. "Possibly someone who knows you."

The pounding of Espen's heart seemed to fill the barn. Someone he knew? Someone he trusted? His head spun. That must explain how Per and Gust were discovered on that deserted road and why the Gestapo had found out about Leif.

"I have more bad news," Tante Marie said. "Sit down. I think I will, too."

They sat down together on the bale of straw.

"It's about Stein . . ." Tante Marie paused, then finished quietly. "He's been killed."

Everything seemed to stop for a moment. The silence of the barn roared in Espen's ears. He thought of the documents, their edges curled with dried blood. Stein's blood? He felt his hands clench into fists. He didn't blame Per and Gust. Everyone knew the Gestapo's methods could be impossible to withstand. They beat prisoners with steel springs, broke their bones, battered their faces, held their heads underwater until they passed out, over and over again. Who knew how he himself would stand up under torture? No, he blamed the informer, the spy. If he ever found out who it was . . .

"Perhaps you should disappear for a time," Tante Marie said. The white strands in her red hair caught the light and glinted like silver threads.

"But," Espen said, "Leif and Ole are gone, and Per and Gust are out of commission. And Stein . . ." He felt his chest tighten, then finished by saying, "Who is left to do the work?"

After the box had been returned to its hiding place under the floor and Tante Marie was back in her warm kitchen, Espen climbed up onto the roof and commenced shoveling. As he scooped up shovelful after shovelful of blindingly bright snow, he wondered who the "shadow" could be. Who was the spy?

Someone from the train station? Or one of the fellows who worked with Ole in the radio shop? Or—Espen stopped to watch a scoop of snow fly off the roof in an explosion of glittering confetti—perhaps someone who worked with Leif in the fish factory? With each shovelful of snow, he thought of another possibility. A neighbor? A friend of the family? One of his old school chums? And with each shovelful, he felt himself digging down closer to the truth, and he wasn't sure he wanted to get there.

Perhaps he had not been "watching with both eyes,"

he thought. "One eye to see; the other to make sense of it," Tante Marie had once said.

Another scoop of sparkling snow flew off the roof. What had he seen that he hadn't made sense of? He'd seen something sparkling, like this, he remembered. Recently. Yes, it had been when he and the other boys were preparing for the airdrop. He'd seen something winking on the far hillside, reminding him of diamonds set against the dark spruce trees. He remembered that he had wondered what it was, but then it had slipped his mind.

What else? What else had he missed? When he'd gone to see Snekker, after the ski race at school, he had heard a noise, like a branch snapping. He hadn't paid enough attention to that, either.

What else? Per had said he'd felt as if he was being watched. What else?

Espen began shoveling with increasing ferocity, digging ever deeper into the core of his memory. Stein was dead. Per and Gust beaten up. Leif and Ole on their way over the mountains. Who was responsible for this? Espen was going to find out. He would find out, and he would even the score.

Back in the house, Espen said, "I'm going to stay."

Tante Marie looked at him, her eyes hot pinpricks on his cold skin. "No matter who the shadow turns out to be," she said, "don't let it eat you up. You must not let bitterness take hold of you."

"How do you keep from being angry and bitter?" Espen cried. "When it doesn't seem to matter what we do? Nothing ever gets better! It just gets worse and worse."

"Anger, hatred, bitterness, fear—those are the emotions that drive the Nazis," Tante Marie said. "That is what has made them the way they are. Don't be swallowed up into their darkness. Whatever else you do, my boy, move toward the light."

The Devil on a Bicycle

ove toward the light. How was he supposed to do that? Espen wondered, as he sped down the hill into the enveloping darkness. His mood was as dark as the mountains, which tonight seemed to loom over the valley and its winding river like hungry trolls. Coasting down the road on a borrowed bike, he could see only darkness and shadows: his own shadow riding a shadow bicycle through the shadows of the tall trees that lined the road. And, perhaps, some shadow he could not see.

He hunched his shoulders against the cold and looked behind him. Was he being followed now?

Why, Espen wondered, of his group, was he the only one who was not in prison or on his way to Sweden? Or dead, he thought, feeling the cold course through him as if through his very veins. He remembered how he had been warned away from Leif's house when the Gestapo had been there. He had also been warned to stay away from Levin's shop when he was carrying the radio. It had been Kjell both times. Why had Kjell been there just then, standing in the shadows as if he'd been waiting for Espen? If Kjell—his friend—had been responsible for what had happened to Stein and Per and Gust but had somehow spared Espen . . . that made him angrier than anything!

The idea of Kjell being the spy dogged him, pedaling after him like the devil on a bicycle.

~—————

"Are you worried about the spy?" Tante Marie had asked him as she jiggled the key in the shed door.

"Of course," he'd said, "but I'll be careful. I'm more worried for my family." His father was taking risks. Even his sister. She'd been feeding prisoners. And she kept a diary, he explained, and he was worried what she wrote in it. Why did she have to do something so frivolous that didn't help anyone yet was still so dangerous?

"'Frivolous'?" Tante Marie wheeled her bike out of the shed. "'Not helping'? Did I hear that from you—Odin?" She stressed his code name. "Do you not remember that your namesake had two ravens whose names were . . ."

"Hugin and Munin," Espen said. "Thought and Memory."

"Very good," Tante Marie said. "Every day, they flew to the four corners of the earth to spy for Odin, and they came back at evening to perch on his shoulders. Then they would whisper into his ears all they had learned. You know what Odin said about them?"

"No, but I have a feeling you are going to tell me," Espen said.

> "Hugin and Munin fly each day,
>   Over the spacious earth,"

Tante Marie recited.

> "I fear for Hugin,
>   That he come not back,
>   Yet more anxious am I for Munin."

"So, what that means is that Odin was more worried about memory than thought?" Espen asked.

"That's the way I'd interpret it," Tante Marie said.

⌐—#—ↄ

Memory! Espen thought now. What was so great about it? Why would anyone want to remember any of this: the food shortages, the confiscations, living in dread of the knock at the door? *Nacht und Nebel,* the Gestapo called it, *Night and Fog.* The knock came in the middle of the night; people disappeared in fog.

Hundreds of people in Oslo had been arrested just for carrying flowers on the king's birthday. A fishing village in the north had been burned to the ground, eighteen of its young men executed and its entire male population sent to concentration camps in Germany. The Gestapo took its wrath out on Milorg and other Resistance groups. Arrests, torture, murders, and executions were happening all over Norway. Many groups had unraveled, including his own.

Nothing he or the larger Resistance movement did seemed to make any difference. Did it matter what he did or didn't do? He couldn't even remember why he had even gotten involved in the first place.

Suddenly, something moved on the road ahead of him. It was so unexpected, it made his heart jump. He slammed on his brakes. There, moving about in the glow of his bike light, were four big black grouse—capercaillie, they were called.

Espen climbed stiffly off his bike and stood watching the elegant birds, with their tail feathers fanned into a regal display, as they calmly pecked gravel by the side of the road. The night was so quiet, he could hear the low chuckling sound the birds made and the scratching of their feet against the gravel. They seemed unconcerned about his presence. They seemed unconcerned about anything. There was no war for them, no war here. For them, all was tranquil.

They didn't even seem cold, Espen thought, shivering. He shoved his hands under his armpits and jumped up and down, trying to get warm.

"Be stronger than the cold," his gym teacher had once said, as Espen and his classmates stood shivering in their gym shorts one early spring day. Tante Marie had once told him he had to be "smarter than the Nazis." Then, recently, she had told him that it wasn't enough to be smarter. "You also have to be *better,*" she'd said.

Stronger. Smarter. Better. Why couldn't he just *be?* Like these birds, pecking away at the side of the road.

He inhaled, gulping in the frosty mountain air as if it was an elixir that could make him stronger, smarter, better. There was a folktale he knew, about a boy who drank from a troll's flask and became as strong as the troll himself, strong enough to slice off the troll's many heads in one blow. He supposed Tante Marie would say that it wasn't enough to be stronger—the boy would also have to be smarter. And better. Otherwise, by drinking the troll's brew, perhaps he had just become a troll himself.

Espen swallowed a few more draughts of the cold air, until his heart felt like it had turned to ice. He would get even with Kjell, he decided. He pulled his collar up against the cold and climbed back onto his bicycle, the wheels ticking like the wheels in his mind, spinning out a plan as he plunged into the darkness.

1944

THOSE WHO DON'T WORK SHALL NOT EAT.

—JOSEF TERBOVEN, REICHSKOMMISSAR FOR NORWAY

Ingrid's Diaries

Every knock on the door now made Ingrid jump. Some of Espen's friends had been arrested, tortured, and sent to a prison camp. One of his old soccer teammates had been killed—shot through the chest by a Gestapo agent. Two others had escaped to Sweden.

Where, Ingrid wondered, was Espen? She had not seen him for weeks, and if their parents knew where he was, they weren't saying.

Her diaries were spread out in front of her on the floor. They had been gifts, given to her each Christmas by her mother, a new one for every new year. Each came in a beautiful leather case with the year printed on the spine. She had loved looking at them all lined up in her bookcase. It made her feel very grown-up.

Ingrid slid each diary into its case and then into an old pillowcase. She hoped her mother wouldn't mind that she was using the pillowcase for this purpose. The latest one, 1943, went in, then '42, '41, and '40. At last, she held her very first diary in her hand. This one, she thought, didn't need to be hidden. This one was from *before*.

She opened it and slid her hand over its smooth pages, pressed her face against the cool interior, held it to her nose and inhaled. Could she smell it—those days gone by? The Christmas goose in the oven? The cardamom bread? The spiced gløgg simmering on the stove? The midsummer feasts of crayfish and shrimp? Butter. Milk. Cream. She ran her tongue around her mouth, trying to remember the thick, sweet, buttery taste of cream, but she could not.

Without her diaries, would she have forgotten everything?

In these pages there were memories of summer days at her grandmother's farm, of crisp fall days when the yellow leaves drifted out of the sky and piled into shining heaps of gold. She remembered how Espen and Kjell had sometimes—

Kjell! She set her book in her lap. She could still picture him as he was then. His confident, easy stride. His kindness to her. Once, she had accidentally dumped her entire basket of strawberries out onto the ground, and he had poured his own into her basket.

When Espen had teased her about a *draug* snatching her out of their rowboat, Kjell had played along with him, but then he assured her with a wink and a shake of his head that there was no *draug*. She had decided then and there that she would marry him when she grew up.

She set aside this one diary and looked at it thoughtfully. She looked, too, at her new 1944 volume, the one her mother had given her just this Christmas, not yet even out of its case. Smiling, she set these two aside. Then she tied a knot in the top of the pillowcase. The ground in the garden was still soft where they had recently dug up some potatoes. She would bury the pillowcase there.

The Hijacking

AKSEL

ksel sat at the breakfast table. He was in a foul mood. There had been more sabotage by Norwegian troublemakers. They hadn't blown up a bridge or a ship or a munitions factory. They hadn't blown up anything at all, but this one still hit hard.

"What's troubling you?" his mother asked.

"The German command finally figured out how to get the lazy Norwegians in line. To get them to sign up for the Labor Service—which, of course, they all should do—they have to get hit where it hurts."

"And where is that?" she asked.

"Their stomachs," Aksel said. "*Wer nicht arbeitet, soll auch nicht essen.*"

"You know I don't understand German," his mother said.

"'Those who don't work shall not eat,'" Aksel translated. "That's a quote from Reichskommissar Terboven. The idea is, if they don't register for the Labor Service, they won't be able to eat: no ration cards." He tore off a chunk of bread and chewed it angrily. "They *should* sign up. It's the *law*." How were the Nazis going to keep order if nobody obeyed the law? The country would fall into chaos.

"I take it something went wrong," his mother said. She set her coffee cup in its saucer.

"Somebody hijacked the ration card truck," he said.

"How on earth did that happen?" she asked.

Aksel almost thought he saw a slight smile flicker on her lips, but he must have imagined it.

"The hijacking . . . ," he began bitterly. He could imagine how it had happened . . .

It would only take a handful of fellows, most of them hiding in the woods or behind boulders, a car stopped in the middle of the road, with two fellows peering under the hood. The driver of the ration card truck stops, waves at them to move their car. They shrug and gesture to the car—"broken down!"—and so the driver gets out and goes over to them to see if he can help . . . while the men hiding in the woods creep out and rush the guard still sitting in the truck. Other men overpower the driver. Both men are tied up.

The Milorg men take the boxes of ration cards out of the truck and load them into their car and drive off to some secret location in the mountains. The boxes of ration cards are then unloaded, and the car is driven away by a single driver, straight into someone's barn, where it is repainted, to reappear later as an entirely different car. In the meantime, *the cards are used to buy food for the men hiding in the mountains, the "Boys in the Woods," as they were known.*

—⫘—

"There must be thousands of the lazy louts hiding up in the mountains by now!" he said out loud.

"Really?" his mother said. "So many!"

"Just to get out of work," Aksel added.

"Who knew the Norwegians could be so lazy! Do you really think that is the main reason?"

"Not you, too!" Aksel cried in exasperation. "Are you going to side with them, too? Along with everybody else?" Aksel glanced at her. She hadn't combed her hair yet this morning and was still wearing her dressing gown.

She sighed and said, "I wish you were more like your father."

"Dead, you mean?"

"No, of course not," his mother replied. "I just meant, he had high ideals."

"I have high ideals!" Aksel insisted.

"Sometimes I think you just like to hurt people," she said.

"I don't *like* to," Aksel said. "It's just *necessary* sometimes."

"Why?" she asked.

"Do you think Father was in Finland being *nice* to people?"

His mother got up from the table, taking her coffee with her.

"He was killing Russians, *Mor*—that's what he was doing there."

"Well, he wasn't killing his own countrymen," she mumbled under her breath.

"What?" Aksel stood up so abruptly, his chair tipped backward.

"All this killing! And misery!" she cried. "Can't it stop? What's it for?"

"If the Norwegians would just . . ."

"No!" She held up her hand. "I don't want to hear it. You and your rationalizing . . . I just don't want to hear it anymore."

"I try to be good to you," he said.

"These are your own countrymen you're abusing," she said. "Your own friends!"

"They were never my friends," he said.

"Can't you feel any compassion, Aksel?" she asked.

"'Close your hearts to pity! Act brutally! The stronger man is right. Be harsh and remorseless. Be steeled against all signs of compassion.'"

"What," his mother whispered, "are you saying?"

"I am merely repeating the words of the Führer, *Mor*," Aksel said. "This is what Hitler has instructed us to do." He went out into the front hall.

"When you lose compassion, you have lost your soul!" she called after him.

Aksel stopped by the mirror in the hall. In the reflection, he could see his mother coming up behind him.

"I have compassion for you," he said. This, he thought, was kind of him to say, because, honestly, she looked terrible.

"Aksel," she said, "you can't be compassionate toward some people but not others. That is not compassion."

He looked at himself in the mirror. Really, he looked quite good, he thought. Like he might catch some criminals today. That would help him with the promotion he wanted. It would take just one brilliant capture, or one brilliant idea, or one brilliant thought. And right then, quite unexpectedly, he had one!

"I just thought of something," he said out loud. "Those ration cards are worthless."

There was no reply. But he hadn't expected one.

"They are no good unless they're stamped. And they weren't. They have to be marked with the stamp from the ration card office if they're to be used. Ha!" He put on his hat, saluted himself, and, on that triumphant note, marched out of the house.

The New Contact

ESPEN

spen tried to appear casual as he strolled along the pier—all while trying to fasten the small pin onto his lapel that would identify him to his new contact. *Another* new contact, he silently groused, glancing around at the few fishermen who stood with their backs to him, their eyes focused on their lines.

The fjord was still and the sun bright. Espen had to squint into the light glinting off the water. Against it, the fishermen appeared as black silhouettes. He didn't like it; he preferred to see peoples' faces.

He trusted no one and suspected everyone. He had not slept at home for weeks, choosing instead to stay with Snekker at Oleanna, or sometimes at friends' homes, or, more and more often, on the couch in Solveig's living room.

But soon he would be in Sweden, he told himself. He had just this one assignment, then his personal assignment, and then to Sweden, where the cities were lit up at night and there was food, plenty of food. He had already planned what he would eat when he got there: soft white bread and butter . . . meatballs and gravy . . . and cake with real whipped cream.

He slid his hand into his secret jacket pocket and touched the folded papers he had put there. The other hidden pocket was reserved for whatever his contact was bringing him.

Where was his contact? He looked at the men on the pier and began to imagine that they were all agents for the Gestapo, dressed as fishermen, and the whole thing was a setup. His contact would identify him; all the fishermen would turn and open fire. His body, pierced with bullet holes, would flop off the dock and into the water, to be eaten by crabs.

He groaned. Not only because of the grisly scenario he'd just imagined for himself, but because his *sister* was now walking toward him down the pier. Ingrid! What was *she* doing here? He had to get rid of her!

"Ingrid!" "Espen!" brother and sister exclaimed simultaneously.

"What are you doing here?" Espen asked.

"What are you doing here?" Ingrid said.

"I asked you first," Espen insisted.

"I asked you at the same time you asked me."

"Well, go home," Espen told her. "You shouldn't be here."

"*You* go home," Ingrid said. "I have . . . business."

"'Business'! What kind of 'business'?"

"It's important. Go away."

"What kind of 'business'?" Espen repeated.

"None of *your* business!"

"I'm not so sure about that," Espen said slowly. Something was dawning on him. This was the girl who had stolen ration cards, after all, and he was pretty sure that what he was picking up from his contact was a ration card stamp.

Ingrid shifted her eyes to his collar, upon which his pin hung lopsidedly. "You?" she said.

He nodded.

She laughed.

He did not. "Ingrid!" he whispered. "You should not be getting involved in this."

"Why not? It looks like you are."

"I'm older than you."

"*Ja?* Well . . . how long have you been doing this?" she said.

"Since . . . the beginning," Espen replied.

"Well, then," she said, "I'm the same age you were when you started."

"That's different."

"Because you're a *boy?*"

"No." He grabbed her by the arm and hurried her to the end of the pier, farther away from the fishermen.

"It's gotten a lot more dangerous," Espen said. "When I started, it was . . . it was almost like a lark. It was fun. But the

Germans were trying to be friendly at first, and they let us get away with things. Not anymore. Now they're like hungry wolves, ready to devour anyone and everyone. Being a cute little girl won't keep you safe."

"Good grief!" Ingrid exclaimed. "I'm not a 'little girl,' Espen! I'm almost *fourteen!*"

"Give me the package," he demanded, "and promise me you won't do anything like this ever again."

"I'll give you the package," she said, "if you'll stop telling me what to do!"

They stared each other down for a few moments. Then Espen grabbed her and pulled her to him in a big hug. He wondered if she could feel his heart pounding.

She slipped the small package into his pocket, then turned and ran away down the pier. He pretended to chase her while she squealed and waved her arms above her head, just as she had when she was little.

Once she was gone, he comforted himself with the knowledge that at least now the stamp was in *his* pocket and not hers. And soon he would deposit it with his Milorg contact.

But first, he wanted to tend to his personal business, and he was angrier than ever because now he had to worry for his sister's safety, too.

He climbed onto his bicycle and pumped hard all the way to Kjell's house. He tore into the yard, skidded on the gravel, and dropped the bike right where it was.

Was this Kjell's house? It looked different than he remembered. But then, he had not stood in front of this house for years. Before that, he had spent many happy hours here. And yet, he had never noticed before how small it was. How plain. How bare. How poor. He had never noticed the peeling paint or the missing shingles.

Hardly anybody had a lot of money, or even very much money. Times were hard, everyone said. Nobody he knew got new clothes or new anything. But why had he never realized just *how* poor Kjell and his grandmother must have been, even before the war?

The door of the house swung open. Kjell's *bestemor* came out onto the stoop, clutching her heavy wool sweater around her. She looked older than Espen remembered, stooped and thin, her white hair floating around her head like wisps of smoke. Her usually friendly face was drawn tight, her eyes narrowed.

"Can I help you?" she said without any warmth.

"It's Espen."

"Oh! Espen!" she cried. "I'm sorry. I didn't recognize you at first. You've grown."

"*Ja,*" he said. "How are you, then?"

"Oh . . ." Her lips compressed in the funny smirk Espen remembered. "I guess I feel more like I do now than I did yesterday."

She hadn't lost her sense of humor, anyway. That was

about the only thing a lot of people had left these days, Espen thought.

"Kjell takes good care of me," she went on. "You know how he is. Would you like to come in?"

Now was his chance, he knew. He could picture the inside of their living room. He would sit down, and she would go into the kitchen to find something for him to eat— she always had—and he would only need a moment to hide the incriminating documents. Then it would just take an anonymous tip to the right people, and Kjell would find out the meaning of trouble.

But he heard himself saying, "*Nei, takk*—No, thanks."

"Shall I tell Kjell you were here?"

"Just give him a message," Espen said. He shoved his hand into his pocket; his fingers curled around the papers there, then crumpled them into a ball. "Tell him . . . I wish him—and you—a happy New Year."

The old woman hobbled down the stairs and walked unsteadily over to him. She placed her hands on either side of his face. "*Tusen takk,* Espen," she whispered. "A thousand thanks. And may the next year be good for you and your family."

He waited until she was back indoors. Then he got onto his bike and pedaled slowly away from the house. He found himself back on the road he had ridden along so often, taking comfort in the familiar effort of climbing the hill. Why, he wondered, hadn't he done what he had set out to do? Had he been too afraid? No, that hadn't been it. Had it been because now Ingrid was involved, and he had to protect her? No, he didn't think so. But he wasn't sure.

Dusk was settling in the valley. Mist rose from the river like smoke, and his steamy breath hung in the still air. He recalled seeing the capercaillies at this spot, a reminder of a peaceful world. That's what he wanted, he remembered. He wanted the world to be like it was for those birds—peaceful, a world without war, where you could go peck gravel by the side of the road if you felt like it, at any time of day or night, and nobody would ask you what you were doing or did you have a permit to do it or who had sent you to do it. That's what he had set out to do, he remembered now, to set the world right, not to tip it more wrong.

No grouse this evening. Just the quiet of his tires ticking against the pavement and his wheels turning and turning like the hands of a clock, spinning the dusk into dark, the dark into dawn, the winter to spring, and the spring into summer.

A Few Beautiful Weeks

spen couldn't have said how it started, exactly, but Solveig began to accompany him on some of his missions. Perhaps it was foolish, but things had settled down and the Germans seemed distracted by other matters. And it was so pleasant to have her company. They carried empty pails, so if anyone stopped them, they could say they were just going to fetch milk from a farm up the way. But no one stopped them. They looked like a young couple running an errand. A young couple in love, maybe.

"Solveig!" her mother would say when they went out. "Where are you going?"

The answer was: hunting mushrooms in the shady forest . . . picking cloudberries on the mountain slopes . . . fishing for trout in the icy streams. And they did do all those things, but only *after* they had completed their missions.

For Espen, his missions with Solveig began to feel like pleasant outings, even—sort of—dates. They joshed and joked and carried on like pals. At first, they pretended that they were a couple, or maybe they just *pretended* that they were pretending.

One day, crossing a stream, Espen reached out his hand to help her. Her hand seemed to fit so nicely into his own that he didn't see a need to let go.

Another day, while they sat watching the river run, Solveig put her head on his shoulder. His arm reached around to encircle her waist, and, he thought, everything was perfect. The way the evening sun glimmered on the water and wavered up the trees that lined the shore—that was perfect, too.

"Everything is perfect right now," he said. "I don't want anything to change. Even the Germans can stay." He laughed.

"I thought you hated them," Solveig said.

"I thought I did, too." Did he need to keep hating them to keep doing what he did?

"Are you going to quit your underground work, then?" Solveig asked, as if reading his thoughts.

"No!" he said. "Of course not." But he felt different, somehow. Who, he wondered, had he been *before?* He couldn't remember the boy he'd left behind. But he felt that, in these long, warm summer days, he was beginning to get a bit of that boy back. Or perhaps he was getting a glimpse of the man he would become.

The days took on a dreamy, kind of sun-drenched magic. Even though horrible things were happening all over the world, still, for a few beautiful weeks in Norway, the sun hung endlessly in the summer sky, lulling Espen into thinking that it would stay that way forever.

1945

INTELLECTUAL GUARDIANSHIP BY PEOPLE WHO ARE
HARDLY MY SUPERIORS IS LIKE SLOW STRANGULATION.
IF THIS IS GOING TO BE OUR CONDITION IN NORWAY,
THEN I SEEK COMFORT IN THE SAYING:
"TO LIVE IS NO NECESSITY."

—JOHAN SCHARFFENBERG,
NORWEGIAN PHYSICIAN AND AUTHOR

The Disguise

I t was winter when Espen got word that Tante Marie was in the hospital, gravely ill. He arrived to find her looking fragile and worn. All the red was gone from her hair, and only the silver, all its luster lost, remained.

"Sit down here," she said.

He pulled a chair up next to her bed.

"I'm not going to last," she said.

"You'll soon be good as new," he assured her. "You just need a good rest."

"Stop talking rubbish and listen to me," she said. "There's not much time for everything I have to say." She coughed, then continued. "You have to retrieve the things from my barn," she went on. "You know where they are. You've been given a kind of promotion, you might say."

"Promotion?" he asked.

She motioned him to put his head down to her. "XU," she whispered.

Espen was so surprised, he couldn't say anything.

"The current XU agent has to be replaced," she said.

"With me?" Espen said. "I'm too young!"

"Young but seasoned," she said. "And trustworthy."

"I can't!" he cried. "The Nazis have really stepped up the labor draft. If I am even seen on the street, they will snag me for sure!"

"What you need is a disguise," said a voice from behind him.

Espen turned to see the doctor standing there.

Disguise. He liked the sound of that.

The doctor told him to wait in his examining room, and he would be with him in a moment.

As he waited, Espen imagined himself being transformed into a handsome, dashing, mysterious spy. He wouldn't look anything like himself. He would sport a pencil-thin mustache. A black trench coat. A fedora. He imagined how the girls would wonder: Who *was* this handsome stranger?

Why, he wondered, was he sitting in a doctor's office instead of visiting a theatrical costumer?

Then the doctor was standing in front of him, arms crossed. He turned his head this way and that, eyeing Espen skeptically. He clucked his tongue and scratched at his two-day growth of board.

"You're a healthy one, aren't you?"

"*Ja,*" Espen replied. "I've always been pretty healthy."

The doctor frowned at him. "Could you at least not sit up so straight? Hunch your shoulders forward."

Espen hunched his shoulders.

"A little coughing, please."

Covering his mouth, Espen let out a polite cough.

"Is that the best you can do?" the doctor asked. He sounded exasperated.

Espen coughed a little harder.

"I'm admitting you to the hospital," the doctor said. "You, young man, are terribly ill."

"I am?"

"We'll do our best to make it seem so." The doctor scrawled something on a chart, then glanced at Espen. "The least you could do is try to look a little sicker."

Look sick? That was going to be his disguise? That wasn't going to get him very far with the girls, and especially Solveig. Espen's heart sank, his shoulders sagged, his face fell.

"That's better!" the doctor chirped. "You look a little pale around the gills now."

Espen groaned.

"Righto! You're getting the hang of it! You'll have a short stay in the hospital to make the medical records convincing." The doctor scribbled his diagnosis on a prescription pad and handed it to Espen. *Tuberculosis,* it read. "You'll be given an official medical certificate exempting you from the Labor Service. Don't you worry," the doctor said, "we'll have you sick in no time."

fortress Norway

Y ou're coming along nicely," the doctor said when Espen saw him next, "and you are ready to be discharged from the hospital. Before you leave, your friend in room 121 would like to see you again."

Espen hurried to Tante Marie's room and opened the door. A man he didn't know stood up from a chair.

"I'm sorry," Espen said, backing out. "I didn't realize you had a visitor."

"Come in," the man said, coming over and closing the door behind Espen.

Espen edged into the room.

"Don't look so worried," Tante Marie said. "This is Taraldsen. He's a good Norwegian."

The man extended a hand, and Espen shook it. "I'm a city engineer here in Lilleby," he said. "Please sit." He gestured to the chair near Tante Marie's bed.

"Good disguise, Odin," Tante Marie croaked. "You look terrible."

"What disguise?" Espen said.

Tante Marie managed a weak chuckle. "Taraldsen is here to discuss a little job for you."

Mr. Taraldsen picked up a cylindrical leather case—Espen recognized it as a case for a fishing rod—and worked at loosening the fasteners as he spoke.

"As you are aware," he said, "we don't expect the war to last much longer. The Allies have won some major victories. Here, in Norway, though, things are a little different."

"Even if or when the Germans surrender elsewhere," Tante Marie said softly, "they might not surrender here."

Taraldsen nodded. "The German army in Norway has been described as 'undefeated and in possession of their full strength,'" he said. "Even if the Wehrmacht in Germany capitulates, will the undefeated army in Norway follow suit? Reichskommissar Terboven has vowed to fight to the last man, and he has nearly four hundred thousand of them on our soil. In addition, there is reason to fear that the Nazis in Berlin will flee to *Festung Norwegen*—'Fortress Norway'—as they call it, and make Norway their bastion. The Allies have indicated they have 'no troops to spare,' and we have about thirty-five to forty thousand Milorg men training in the mountains. You can see the issue, I think. So . . ."

After a moment, Taraldsen pulled the sections of a fishing rod out of the case and continued. "We can only prepare for the worst and do what we can."

"And . . . ?" Espen said, a little puzzled. The hospital was an odd place to assemble a fishing pole.

"As you probably realize, the headquarters for Fortress

Norway is right here in Lilleby." Taraldsen pulled a tightly rolled sheet of paper from the leather case. "Our sources tell us that this garrison is in direct communication with Hitler."

He unrolled the paper and spread it on the bed. Espen saw immediately that it was a map of Lilleby. "Sorry, Tante Marie, do you mind?" Taraldsen said.

"Not at all," she replied. "I'll think of it as practice."

"Practice?" Espen asked.

"Soon I really *will* be under Lilleby," she said, chuckling.

Espen didn't care for the joke, and he told her so; then he helped her sit up so she could see the map that draped over her bedcover.

"Here is the area." Taraldsen traced the area with his finger. "They have requisitioned the tourist hotel and the houses that surround it, rudely expelling the families that live in them."

Espen nodded. He had heard this.

"These three sides are completely surrounded with barbed wire," the engineer went on, "and the whole area is patrolled by armed guards, of course. This fourth side, which is heavily wooded, steep, and rugged, has not been fenced. This may be a way you can enter."

"Enter?" Espen squeaked.

"Oh, did I forget to say that? You're to make a map of the compound, as detailed a map as possible. For that, you will have to get inside."

The problem, as Espen saw it, was not getting *inside* but getting back *outside*.

"We need you," Taraldsen went on, "to gather every speck of information you can: the location of the barracks, officers' quarters, POW camp, weapons depots, bunkers, guardhouses, pipelines, and electrical generators. Most especially the communications bunker. You will bring all this information to my office in the post office building, and we will set it all down on this map."

There was silence in the room as Espen absorbed all he had been told. Finally, he asked, "Any suggestions about how to go about it?"

"That is up to you," the engineer said.

"Up to me!" Espen cried. "But I have no idea!"

Tante Marie coughed out a little laugh. "You just got a disguise. Use it."

"It's not like I'm suddenly invisible!" Espen said.

"You'll come up with something." Tante Marie tipped her head to indicate the table next to her bed. "Now, reach into that drawer. There's something in there for you."

Espen opened the drawer, immediately noticing the roll of bills. Tentatively, he picked it up.

"That," she said, "is escape money, should you need it. Two hundred and fifty *kroner*—fifty *kroner* for each of the five guides you'll require to get to Sweden. Should you have to flee, give the entire amount to the first guide. He'll distribute the rest to the others."

Espen stared at the money in his hand. How could Tante Marie still be thinking of his welfare? He glanced out the window, where the sky was steel gray. The wind must be strong, he thought, because the bare branches of the trees rocked and swayed.

"To live is no necessity," Johan Scharffenberg had said, if it meant living under Nazi rule. Norwegians had embraced the sentiment, risking their lives every day to undermine the Nazis in any way they could. And they kept on no matter how bad it got; they hung on until there was sometimes nothing left but the will to hang on. Why?

Hope, he supposed. Hope, like the glimmer of sun that breaks through the shadow on the mountain. Hope and courage and will. Or perhaps it was just sheer will.

He looked back at Tante Marie. "I'm glad the Gestapo didn't get you," he said.

She managed a weak smile. "Something else in there for you, too," she said.

Espen looked in the drawer. "The false teeth or the compass?" he asked.

"Whichever will be most useful to you," she whispered.

"I'll take the compass, then," he said. "And, Tante Marie, thank you for everything."

She turned her head and looked at him. The fire in her eyes had died to embers. "You have a good compass already," she said. "Right here." She laid her hand on her chest, over her heart. And closed her eyes.

The Gudbrandsdal Method

ig a tunnel? Steal a Wehrmacht uniform? Dress in black and sneak in at night?

They were all bad ideas, doomed to failure. It seemed impossible, this mission he'd just been given. It felt like a sure prison sentence or, more likely, a death sentence. He would manage to get inside only to be arrested, taken to a Gestapo prison, and shot. Or, worse, tortured until he revealed the names of his contacts. And *then* shot. In any case, the inevitable outcome was good-bye. Good-bye, Solveig. Good-bye, *Mor* and *Far*. Good-bye, Ingrid.

He felt he could deal with the fear, but he became so sad, he could hardly bear it. *Well,* he decided, *if that's the way it is to be, I'm not about to die without going home one last time.* Just to breathe in the smell of home, of family, of happier days, of ordinariness. He wanted to smell the pipe smoke on his father's coat as he passed the hall closet, hear the steady ticking of the living room clock and the comforting creak of the wood floor as he walked through to the kitchen . . . The kitchen! Maybe it would be filled with baking. His mother might have gotten hold of some real cream and would be whipping it into soft peaks when he walked in. She would hand Espen the beater to lick. *Oh! For just one piece of cream cake before he died!* Was that too much to ask?

He found himself on his own doorstep; the window was open. He was touched that his mother still did this, even though it had been weeks since he'd last been home. He stepped into the quiet of an empty house.

He walked past the closet—the smell of pipe smoke only a memory, tobacco also only a memory—and then he was in the kitchen.

There was no cake cooling on the counter, no bowl of whipped cream, real or otherwise, standing at the ready, and nothing to smell or eat, either, from the looks of it. Just a note on the counter—*Ingrid, please scrub the potatoes for supper*—and a sinkful of potatoes in need of scrubbing.

Well, Espen thought, he had wanted ordinariness. What was more ordinary than scrubbing potatoes?

He rolled up his sleeves and began his task, with only the ticking of the grandfather clock to accompany him. Solemnly, it had ticked away the years of the Occupation, years that should have been filled with parties and holidays, Christmas cookies and birthday cakes. He should have been a kid just growing up, worrying about girls and soccer games and about the grade he'd gotten on his latest exam. Instead, he worried about getting arrested and tortured or having the Gestapo come to his house in the middle of the night.

He heard the door slam and the thud of a bag being plunked down in the entryway, then the click of heels in the hall.

Some things about these years he wouldn't replace, he thought. Even ordinary, everyday moments like this one seemed distilled—distinct, concentrated, somehow. The afternoon sun streaming in through the kitchen window, the red of the potatoes, their skins glistening, the white flesh beneath so bright—colors were more vibrant, sweetness more sweet, feelings so much more intense. He did, he had to admit, feel intensely alive.

He'd learned a lot in these nearly five years, but the most important thing he'd realized was that of all the feelings that could course through his being in a single afternoon—anger, bitterness, sorrow, fear, longing, hunger (of course), and hate—love was the one that had the most power; it was the one feeling he hoped to cling to through his life, even if his life was to last only one day longer. He loved Solveig, his parents, his beautiful country, freedom, cream cake, and, right now, his sister, who was standing in the doorway, her cheeks flushed with cold, her eyes wide with surprise.

"Espen!" she said. "You look terrible!"

"Thank you," Espen said. "Same to you."

She gave him a kiss on the cheek. "What's wrong with you?"

"Tuberculosis," he said.

Her hand sprang away from him.

"Not really," he added. "It's a sort of disguise."

"Ohhh," she said. "What are you doing now?"

"Scrubbing potatoes," he said.

"I can see that," she said. "I mean, what are you up to now?"

"Nothing much," he answered. "Avoiding the Labor Service."

Ingrid opened the icebox and stared inside for a few moments, then shut the door and sat down at the kitchen table. She cocked her head and looked at him sideways. "I don't believe you."

Espen made a face at her.

"That completes the look!" she said. "You've always had a talent for looking a little foolish. Now you look like a half-wit. Is that your coat in the hall?"

Espen nodded. Solveig had given him a raggedy old coat. She said it made him look even more bedraggled.

Ingrid laughed. "With that coat on, I bet you look like a quarter-wit!"

He looked at her over his shoulder and waggled his eyebrows.

"So . . . ," Ingrid said, nibbling at her fingernails. "What are you up to, really?"

Espen hesitated, then said, "I have an assignment that I'm a little boggled by. I'm not quite sure how to go about it."

"Well," she said, "you know what *Far* would say."

"Use the Gudbrandsdal Method," Espen replied. In the window's reflection, he could see Ingrid nodding.

Espen looked at the potato in his hand. He thought about the potatoes in a box in the basement and more potatoes under the coverlet of snow in the garden. He remembered how Ingrid had fed the prisoners some years before. Those thoughts brought him back to the Gudbrandsdal Method: the simplest way.

The Potato Spy

spen made a wide circle through the woods around the compound so he could come in from the forested hillside—the one side without barbed wire. He reached into his pocket and touched the doctor's certificate he carried there as if it were a magic talisman.

He was ready. He had practiced making his stride exactly one meter long. Ingrid had used a tape measure as he strode around the backyard. She coached him on looking idiotic, stupid, and very, very ill. And then she had cooked up a big batch of potatoes, drained them, and put them in a paper bag, which he now carried under his arm.

"Look confident," she'd said. "No—not confident. Look sick. And idiotic. Above all, idiotic."

Now, as if diving off the high board, he launched himself out of the woods and plunged into the compound, snuffling, sneezing, and coughing out little snatches of folk tunes.

Were there guards watching? he wondered as he stumbled (one meter per stumble) into the main part of the camp. He didn't know. In order to maintain his disguise, he needed to seem unconcerned about such things. If he appeared to be looking for danger, he would look suspicious.

He scuttled close enough to several buildings to read the names of the officers residing there. He repeated the names in his head over and over until he was sure to remember them, so he could write them down later, along with the numbers and the locations of the buildings.

Espen stood and watched a crew of prisoners digging a trench. How they could work at all was a wonder—they were as fragile as skeletons. He was wondering what the trench was for when one of them looked up, saw him and the sack he was holding, and nudged the fellow next to him. They and some others left their work and walked up to him, their hands outstretched. Others followed.

Espen reached into his sack and put a still-warm potato into each hand. He knew he should be looking over their shoulders at the compound or watching for guards, but instead he found himself thinking of Ingrid and how she had fed sandwiches to the prisoners. Her act of kindness, he realized now, had been a powerful act of resistance. It contradicted everything the Nazis stood for. Perhaps, over time, ordinary acts of kindness could turn the Nazi ideology to dust. For this moment, anyway, it had.

Then, out of filthy pockets came offerings from the prisoners, beautifully carved trinkets of all shapes and sizes: wooden crosses, animal figurines, spoons, toys, a wondrous bird with delicately carved wings.

Then he saw the guard. A guard with a machine gun, who, for a moment, stared at him.

Now we're all done for, Espen thought. He held his breath, waiting for a shouted "*Achtung!*" or the thumping of boots or even the sudden rattle of machine-gun fire.

He gazed down at the carved bird, its fragile wings outstretched, ready to take flight. *This is the image I will take with me to heaven,* he thought.

But the guard did something Espen was not expecting: he turned his back.

Espen set the sack of potatoes onto the ground and disappeared into the forest.

Hurrying down the hill toward town, he remembered when Ingrid had said that most of the German soldiers were just boys—like Norwegian boys, decent kids caught up in an unhappy world. Confused or conscripted, what did it matter? They didn't really want to shoot anyone. Maybe she was right. At least about this particular soldier.

Espen returned to the compound several more days, each time with potatoes, and each time he came back to town with more and more of the compound etched into his mind. Later, everything he saw was put down on paper, including the names of the officers, their living quarters, the layout and the purpose of all the buildings. There was just one thing he hadn't found yet: the exact location of the communications center. The most important piece of information.

Each day, Ingrid helped Espen scrub and cook another batch of potatoes. "How long are you going to keep doing this?" she asked. She didn't look at him but stared into the pot of boiling water. "You might be pushing your luck."

"Today is the last time. I promise," he said.

"Good," she answered, turning to him. "Let's celebrate, then. There's a party tonight. Will you go with me?"

A party, Espen thought. How long had it been since he'd been to a party?

"Please?" Ingrid said.

If all went well today, he'd be finished with his task. It would be nice to celebrate. "All right," he said. "Sounds like fun."

It was a cold, crisp day. The sky was as blue as a Danish plate, and new snow covered the ground like a freshly ironed tablecloth. Espen made his way through the birch grove below the compound, gradually assuming his coughing-sputtering-mumbling-stumbling disguise.

He sang a little folk tune, and by the time he reached the camp, he was so transformed, he wondered if even his mother would recognize him.

A few prisoners working in the yard lifted their heads when he came in. They recognized him. He felt a knot develop in his stomach. He was too recognizable; he realized it, but it was too late. He was here now.

"*Paul let his chickens run out on the hillside,*" he coughed and sang, "*Over the hill they went tripping along.*"

He bumbled his way around the back of the main buildings. "*Paul understood by the way they were acting; he sensed a warning that something was wrong.*" Espen glanced behind him. "*Cluck, cluck, cluck! The chickens are cackling.*"

Suddenly, his surroundings came into sharp focus. The moment, and everything around him, seemed to condense into a small pinprick of light in his head: Danger. He could feel it.

Then he heard it.

"Halt!" a voice barked.

"*Paul made a rush for the top of the hillside,*" Espen sang quietly. "*There was a fox with a hen in his paw.*"

Footsteps crunched on the gravel behind him.

"*Paul took a rock, and with madness he threw it, Striking directly the fox in the jaw.*" He considered turning and flinging a potato at whoever was behind him, but throwing a rock at a fox and throwing a potato at a German soldier were two rather different offenses.

The person said something in Norwegian. In the local dialect. Espen recognized the voice. It was someone he knew.

Fox and Hen

ksel recognized the guttersnipe who was stumbling around the compound in a too-large coat. Of course he did. He couldn't think of the name, but he knew who it was: the kid who had tossed him the jellyfish soccer ball years before.

The Occupation had been hard on everyone, but it seemed to have been extra hard on this poor crackpot. Since Aksel had seen him last, he'd grown taller, if not any heavier. But he looked sick. Sick, stupid, and half-mad. He looked, to Aksel, like someone who should be put out of his misery.

Aksel flipped open the holster on his side.

Then it occurred to him that perhaps this sap was not as stupid and sick as he seemed. Maybe he was faking it. What was he doing here, really? He did not belong here and had no reason to be here.

Aksel fingered the butt of his pistol.

On the other hand, Aksel knew that he himself had no legitimate business here, either. He was just snooping around, trying to find out how the war was going. He knew what the Nazi-run radio and newspapers said, and he knew it was all propaganda. He suspected that the addle-brain standing in front of him knew more about the truth of what was happening in the war than most of the German soldiers, because he would have been listening to illegal radio broadcasts and reading underground newspapers.

So, he was in a predicament. If he arrested this fellow—possibly a spy—if he hauled him in and interrupted the commandant's lunch, it was possible, just possible, that Aksel would be applauded and perhaps promoted again. Maybe even given a job that would take him away from his hometown and the derisive attitudes of the towns-people.

However, if it turned out that the chump really *was* an idiot and Aksel had interrupted the commandant's lunch for nothing, then it would surely be brought to the commandant's attention that Aksel had no business being at the compound in the first place. If so, Aksel would, once again, be made a laughingstock. Much like the time he had failed to catch Leif after a wild-goose chase. And the time he had lost the important papers taken from Stein's house. And the time the schoolchildren had refused to participate in the ski race that it had been his job to organize. And also the time everyone had quit the soccer team.

Aksel would relish the opportunity to get rid of this

thorn in his side. He could think of it as a way to even the score. Now, what *was* his name?

⬤—‖—⬤

They were standing so close that Espen could smell the damp wool of Aksel's locust-green uniform and hear the creak of his shiny black leather boots as he shifted his weight.

As he waited for Aksel to shoot him in the back, Espen noticed something. What the prisoners were working on was a trench. A trench in which cables were being laid . . . cables that might well run to a communications center. Which was the single most important thing he needed to find. If only the earth would open and swallow Aksel right now.

But it did not.

"Turn around," Aksel commanded.

Espen turned.

"What's in the sack?"

"'tatoes," Espen mumbled. He held the bag out to Aksel.

Aksel looked into the bag and handed it back. "How is it you are not at work?" he said. "Let me see your identity card."

". . . my pocket," Espen mumbled.

Aksel waved the gun at him to go ahead and produce it.

Espen stuck his hand into his pocket and gripped his medical exemption. The magic talisman, he hoped. He handed the paper to Aksel.

Aksel stared down at it while keeping his gun trained on Espen. Then he handed it back and glowered at his former teammate.

It was a look Espen remembered, a look that used to make his stomach churn. Nothing good ever came of it. Well, Espen thought, it was Aksel's look, and he could keep it.

"*Never again will that hen ever cackle,*" Espen stuttered in a singsong voice while turning around. "*Never again will she let out a peep. Now I must go to the mill and do grinding . . .*"

He expected at any moment to hear the pop of a Luger or the rattle of machine-gun fire. *Let him shoot me in the back, if he has to shoot me. He should have to be the coward I know he is,* he thought. Nevertheless, he began to walk away, alternately coughing and singing, "*'Pshaw!' said Paul, 'Now why should I worry? A brave tongue and courage have helped quite a few.'*"

Then he heard footsteps and sensed a different presence behind him. When he glanced over his shoulder, he saw that he was being followed by dozens of prisoners, floating between him and Aksel like a band of raggedy angels.

Aksel watched Espen walk down the hill, past the trench the prisoners were digging. He saw the prisoners leave their work and tag along behind the young man in the tattered coat. Aksel followed at a distance, concealed from view by the prisoners. *Give him a little lead,* Aksel thought. *See where he goes.* He watched him climb down an embankment and disappear from view.

As soon as he had seen the name on the identity card, Aksel remembered it: Espen. Espen the goalie who had tossed him the jellyfish ball. Espen, whose fault it was that the others had laughed at Aksel and never taken him seriously.

It was probably Espen's fault that the soccer team had stalked off the field the day he'd been made captain. Who knew if it wasn't also his idea to not finish the ski race? It might even have been Espen who had convinced the others to get involved with Milorg. And he'd probably been the one who warned Leif to get away before Aksel could catch him.

Aksel came to the edge of the embankment, then scrambled over it and down the slope. He turned to see a cave dug out of the side of the hill—a bunker filled with communications equipment. A glance inside was all it took for Aksel to see desks equipped with radio sets and telephones and typewriters.

"*Achtung!*" a voice within called out, and Aksel scurried away.

Espen was long gone. No doubt he had already ducked under the barbed wire and down the steep hill.

But now Aksel was absolutely sure that Espen was a spy. Yes, Aksel thought, and the root of all his troubles. But he would get him. One way or another, he would catch Espen. Maybe not now, but soon enough.

The Map

eep in the forest, Espen ripped off his coat and buried it in the snow, raked his fingers through his hair, then hurried to the engineer's office.

Taraldsen slid the map out of a drawer, and he and Espen hunched over it. Together, they marked each thing that Espen had discovered until they had completed a precise map of the compound.

"It's very good," Taraldsen said. "Every detail—perfect! The map will be sent by courier to Sweden, and from there to the right hands."

Espen told the engineer he had been recognized.

"You'd better disappear right away," the man advised.

Espen agreed that the time had come. He would go . . . soon. First, there was the party he had promised to attend with Ingrid, and he intended to go. But before that, he would go see his father.

His father looked up from his desk when Espen walked in.

"I think I may have to 'disappear' for a while," Espen said.

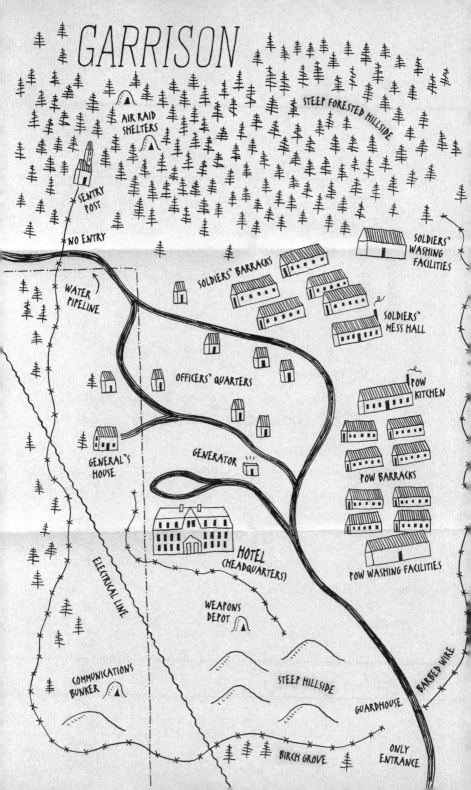

His father nodded. Espen saw his jaw twitch with pain—possibly from the stomach ulcer that plagued him all the time now. Then he walked over to Espen and placed both hands on his shoulders. "If I should be taken as a hostage for you," he said, "the worst thing you could do would be to come out of hiding to set me free."

Espen couldn't speak for a moment. There was, he thought, too much to say—or what there was to say could not be said but only felt. They clasped hands; then Espen said good-bye, turned, and walked swiftly away.

After the Party

Ingrid and Espen strolled through the dark streets on their way home from the party later that evening. It was late. So late, and Espen was so tired. Too tired to try to leave town that night. Tomorrow would be soon enough, he thought. Besides, he really wanted to say good-bye to Solveig before he left for what might be a very long time. She hadn't been at the party.

"I was thinking of stopping home for some things," he said, "but I don't want to worry *Mor*." He could get his radio and his "escape money" from the house in the morning, he decided.

"What things?"

"Just a couple of things," Espen said. He wished he could share with Ingrid all that had happened, but she already knew more than she should. Of course, he longed to have someone to confide in. Sometimes he was so exhausted by all the responsibility and tension, it would be good just to get it off his chest. Ingrid would help him want to keep going. She'd be proud of him if she knew all the things he'd done.

She looked at him as if she was going to cry. "Espen . . . ," she said, "you know I can keep secrets. You know I will never tell anybody anything. No matter what."

"I know," he replied, "but there's no reason for you to know."

"At least tell me where you are staying," she said.

Espen sighed. Tomorrow he would be gone, and then it wouldn't matter. "At Solveig's," he answered.

"Oh!" Ingrid exclaimed. "There's a *lot* I don't know."

Espen laughed and strolled away, then called back, "Wasn't the cake just grand?" Their laughter pealed through the empty streets.

Espen crept into the Dahls' house quietly. It was late. Solveig and her parents were sure to be asleep. He could say good-bye in the morning.

He did what he did every single night: he stuffed all his clothes and his shoes into his rucksack and set it next to the couch. That way he could, in one swift movement, grab his sleeping bag off the couch with one hand and his rucksack with the other and race down the stairs to the basement. And, if necessary, from there out the storm cellar door into the night.

Then he climbed into his sleeping bag and enjoyed the delicious feeling of a warm bag and a tired body. It was late; the clock in the hall ticked sleepily. He thought for a few moments about the party. A lot of his friends from school had been there—minus his soccer teammates. Their absence made the party bittersweet. Like a lot of things nowadays, Espen thought. But there had been some food, and that was nice: herring and brown bread, and someone had gotten hold of a nice chunk of Jarlsberg cheese.

But the crowning glory had been the cake. Ingrid's friend, Caroline, had been so thrilled to find a chocolate cake with white frosting in the bakery downtown, and it did look delicious. She made a little performance out of cutting into it and making sure each person got an equal-size slice. Espen's mouth had started watering right away, but he managed to keep from eating until everyone had a slice. Finally, Caroline said, "*Vær så god*," and Espen, along with everyone else, attacked the dessert. But, after the first bite, there had been a moment of silence. The guests looked at one another.

"What on earth *is* it?" Caroline said, and they'd all burst out laughing.

"Rye bread . . . I think," Nils answered.

"With beaten egg whites for frosting!" Kari added.

It was terrible. But, of course, they ate it anyway.

Espen fell asleep with a smile on his face, determined to have a dream of *real* cake. He never would have dreamt what was transpiring at his own house at that very moment.

Unexpected Company

Ingrid walked home, smiling. She was tickled about Espen and Solveig and was giggling when she opened the front door. Her laughter stuck in her throat when she was seized by two Gestapo officers. Two others stood with their guns trained on her parents.

Her parents sat on the couch, her mother in her dressing gown, her father still in his work shirt. Her mother was pale but looked stoic and determined. Ingrid could see that they were trying to stay calm, but she felt a kind of panic welling in her chest. She tried to take a breath but couldn't—she felt as if she had been plunged into an icy stream.

"Good evening, miss," said the older of the two officers. He looked newly shaved, with a clean shirt. As if he had been planning to attend a party. Then she thought: Maybe *this* was the party. "We have been waiting for you," he said, "and your brother."

Ingrid said nothing in response to the officer, so he added, "He isn't with you?"

"No," she said.

"But he was with you earlier?"

Ingrid's mind raced. There were a lot of people at the party. Anyone might have told them he had been there. "Yes," she said.

"And where was that?"

"A party."

"Where was the party?"

"He wouldn't be there anymore. He left."

"Ah, and where did he go?"

"I don't know."

"Perhaps if you think for a moment, something will occur to you."

Ingrid was silent.

"You will show this young man your brother's bedroom." He gestured toward a person standing behind her, and Ingrid turned to see a fellow dressed in plainclothes standing in the shadows. He looked familiar—Norwegian. Did she know him from somewhere? He wasn't one of Espen's close friends. He had never been on the soccer team. She was sure of that, but, still, he seemed familiar.

The officer motioned to the staircase. She felt like saying, no, she didn't think she would like to show anybody anything, but then she felt the very hard barrel of a gun pressed into the small of her back.

Ingrid started up the stairs with the young Norwegian fellow following. Each step was agony.

Espen. What might be in his bedroom?

This young man. How did she know him?

Her diaries. She took mental inventory of where each one was.

They walked into Espen's bedroom, and the young man immediately began going through the desk drawers. It didn't take him long to come upon a cash box, which, when opened, revealed 250 *kroner*. He held it out to her.

"Where did he get this?" he said.

"I don't know," she said. This was true, though she now guessed that this was what Espen wanted to come back to the house to retrieve. "He works at the station sometimes. I suppose he earned it."

The boy put the money back into the box. *Well!* Ingrid noted. *A shred of decency!*

Then he found a small pocket radio and showed that to Ingrid.

"I didn't know he had one," Ingrid said. That was also true.

Next, the young man picked up a photo album and opened it. "Please point out your brother's girlfriend," he said.

Ingrid walked slowly to the album, trying to think what to say if there was a photo of Solveig in the book. The question of who this fellow was nagged at her. She was sure she knew him from somewhere.

He turned the pages. There were photos of Espen as a young boy. Of Espen and Ingrid together as babies, as children, as youngsters. Ingrid's mind raced. If he didn't find anything here, would they search her room? She thought again of her diaries.

The years passed by in the photos. Here was Espen in his scout uniform with his troop. Ingrid's hand paused over the photo, and she raised her head, turning to look at the young man next to her.

For a brief moment, their eyes met. Then he averted his gaze and flipped the page quickly.

That was it! He had been a scout with Espen. He had been a friend of Espen's. Just a few years earlier. And now he was hunting Espen like an animal! Ingrid wanted to fly at him, to choke him, kick him, anything! Her anger rose in her throat. How could he turn against his own countrymen—his own *friends*?

She could see his ears grow pink as she stared at him.

"The girlfriend, please," he said. "Please point out his girlfriend." He brandished his gun at her and tried to look stern.

Now that she really looked at him, she could see that he was nervous and ill at ease. *He doesn't want to be doing this,* she thought. She resisted the impulse to feel sorry for him. He *should* be unhappy, she thought.

The boy flipped through the album rapidly and arrived at the recent pages. There were photos of Ingrid's birthday party last year. Of Grandmother knitting. Of Mother in the garden. There was not a single photograph of Solveig.

"Even if he had a girlfriend," Ingrid said, "he wouldn't tell me."

"Where has he gone?"

"I have no idea," Ingrid said. "Do you think he tells his *sister* anything?" She heard her voice talking, doing her best to maintain a friendly, even jovial, tone, while her mind clicked and whirred. How could she get a warning to Espen?

The young Norwegian tucked the radio under his arm and gestured to Ingrid to leave the room. They walked down the hall and were almost past Ingrid's room when he said, "Stop."

She stopped.

"Is this your room?" he said.

She nodded. He gestured for her to enter, and she stood staring at the window, though the shades were drawn, while he looked all around the room. She would not, she willed herself, look at the bookshelf where the diary labeled 1939 was stowed. He had seen it, though, and he picked it up and waggled it at her.

"What is this?" he asked.

She held her voice steady. "It's a diary."

"Where are the others?" he said.

"Others?"

"From more recent years," he said.

"I gave up diary writing after that," she said.

"My sister keeps a diary," the fellow said, "and she keeps it . . ." He stalked over to the bed and plunged his hand under her pillow. "Ah!" he said, holding up the diary she had stashed there. "Under her pillow." He turned the spine to face him and read, "1945."

"Where are the others? 1940 through 1944?" he asked.

"I burned them," she said. "I don't want to remember those years."

"And this year?"

"Is different," she said. He would know what that meant. All anyone talked about these days was how the Germans were losing on all fronts. It just made them meaner than ever, but, still, her countrymen were cautiously happy, knowing the war was somehow going to come to an end— maybe soon.

He took the 1945 diary and gestured for her to move ahead of him out of the room. Once downstairs, the young man gave the radio and the diary to the Gestapo officer, who showed his tobacco-stained teeth in what Ingrid supposed was intended to be a smile. The officer handed the items to one of the other men and turned to her.

"Now, then, why don't you tell us where your brother is?" the Gestapo officer said. He was no longer smiling.

"I told you, I don't know," Ingrid said.

"You were just with him." The man slid his arm around her shoulders almost gently, then placed his hand on the back of her neck. Her skin prickled.

She could see her parents' faces: her mother's hand to her mouth, her eyes welling with tears; her father's teeth clenched in anger.

The officer had moved so that he stood slightly behind her. "I'm quite sure if you think hard enough, you can come up with some idea," he said.

She shook her head. His fingers closed around the back of her neck and squeezed.

"Perhaps now you remember?" he said.

"I don't know," she said firmly.

She felt both of his hands around her neck now, choking her.

"I don't know!" she cried, when he let up for a moment.

His fingers squeezed tighter, choking her, then released. "I don't know!" she gasped. Again and again he gripped her throat and then released it, long enough for her to cry out, "I don't know! I don't know!"

The Knock
at the Door

ESPEN

et up! Go downstairs," Solveig said, shaking Espen. "Hurry!"

Espen leapt off the couch, gathered up his rucksack and his sleeping bag, and rushed down to the basement. At the bottom of the stairs, he climbed into his pants and realized with horror that he had only one shoe. The other one must have fallen out of his rucksack. That meant that one of his shoes was lying out in plain sight. His stomach lurched; he raced to the storm door.

Someone moved about at the top of the stairs.

The latch jiggled noisily in Espen's hand, but the door wouldn't seem to open.

"Espen," he heard. He turned to see Mrs. Dahl standing there. "It's all right. It's your friends."

Espen climbed the stairs to find his neighbor Kari and her boyfriend, Nils, standing in the living room.

"Oh, Espen!" Kari said, breathlessly. "We came to ask Solveig if she knew where you were."

"Well, here I am," Espen said.

"It's lucky we found you," Kari said, "because the Gesta-po's at your house. We think they're waiting for you. We heard—" Kari stopped abruptly. Out of the corner of his eye, Espen caught a glimpse of Solveig shaking her head at Kari.

"You heard what?" Espen said.

"We heard . . . some noise," Kari finished.

Espen's throat felt thick. "What kind of noise?"

"Never mind about that," Solveig said. "You have to get going—fast!"

But Espen's whole body, like the arrow on a compass, swung toward home. "I have to go home," he said.

Solveig grasped his arm. "You know that's not a good idea. You've got to get away—now!" She held out his shoe. "Are these the only shoes you have?"

Espen nodded dumbly, his head throbbing. "My boots are at home," he said. "I changed into these for the party."

"Well, put them on," she said. "It's the best we can do for now."

Solveig helped Espen into his shoes while the others stood over him, giving instructions. ". . . Soria's farm . . . safe for a short time . . . figure out what to do . . ."

Espen watched Nils's mouth moving. He imagined what was happening at home. It was all his fault! "My family . . ." he said.

"Does Ingrid know where you are?" Kari asked.

Espen nodded. Why had he told her? He had endangered her, and Solveig and Solveig's family, too. Even Kari and Nils now.

"She won't say anything—I'm sure of it," Espen said.

Nils started to say, "You know the tactics of the Gestap—"

But Solveig interrupted him, "Of course she won't say anything! But, in any case, you have to go. It's not safe here any longer."

"If I go home, the Gestapo will take me and leave my family alone."

"Will you stop talking and hurry up?" Solveig said, cramming Espen's hat onto his head.

Nils and Kari walked ahead of Espen to the edge of town to make sure the coast was clear. He thanked them numbly and stumbled across the fields to Soria's farm. His shoes kept filling with snow, and he finally stopped and took them off. Then he trudged along in his stocking feet, across fields awash in moonlight, each step punching another dark hole into the snow. The snow was loud, chattering at him. *Yakkity-yak-yak,* like old ladies at a coffee party.

"If you must talk so much, tell me what has happened at my house," he said, in case the gossipy old ladies had news. "Tell me if my family is safe."

But the snow had nothing useful to say; it just whined and complained underfoot.

Outside Espen's House

AKSEL

ksel clenched the steering wheel in his hands and stared down the street in the direction of the house. He should have been in there, in the house. His superior had roughed up the girl, the sister. He'd known that's how it would go. He had heard her yelling. With the window rolled down, he could hear her even from inside the car. The kid, Espen, wasn't home. Aksel was supposed to keep an eye out for him, but he knew the rascal wasn't going to show up. The Gestapo could wait there all night—and probably would. Those Gestapo men were going to botch it, and somehow or other Aksel would be blamed. He could see *that* coming.

He was tired of being blamed for everything that went wrong, and tired of not having a chance to be the front man. This, for example: being made to sit in the car while someone else did the interrogating. Like the flunkie they'd dug up—some old scouting buddy of Espen's—who was in there now, snooping around, while he, Aksel, had to sit in the car. Neither Mr. High-and-Mighty-Gestapo-Man nor that stupid Boy Scout was going to get a thing out of the sister—Aksel knew that much.

In the meantime, Espen was probably hightailing it out of town. Where was he now? Aksel wondered. Crouched in the back of a truck, covered by a tarpaulin, bumping along winding country roads? Or on his way to the coast to catch a ride on a fishing trawler to the Shetland Islands? Or was he strapping on a pair of skis and starting over the mountains toward Sweden?

Aksel closed his eyes, trying to picture the scene. Espen would probably be hiding somewhere until arrangements could be made. Where?

As soon as he was released from this doomed endeavor, Aksel could get to work on really catching Espen, even if he didn't have official orders. He would need some help. But he knew where to get it.

High Country

ESPEN

1t had been a long, uphill climb, and Espen paused to catch his breath. The undulating line of mountains ahead of him looked like waves rolling all the way to Sweden, a kind of ocean of white. Yet not white, exactly. Now, in the moonlight, the landscape was a luminous blue.

The skiing was tough. His wax was bad, and a thin layer of ice had collected on the underside of his skis, which made gliding difficult. Every little while, he and his guide, code-named Haakon, had to stop and scrape the stuff off. They had stopped yet again when Espen looked back at their ski tracks unraveling behind them like endless purple ribbons.

"Do you think we're being followed?" he said.

Haakon shrugged. "Who knows? Not much to do about it but keep going." He had taken one ski all the way off and now scraped at the ice with his knife, cursing under his breath. When his arm was raised, his jacket inched up and caught on the butt of a Colt .32 sticking out of his belt. "If the Germans are following us," he went on, throwing his ski down, then stepping into it, "they're having the same trouble with their skis that we are, so I wouldn't worry."

"I suppose they might have better wax," Espen said.

Haakon snorted. "Germans? Ha! I doubt it." He slipped the straps of his poles over his mittens. "For all the years they've been occupying Norway, you'd think they could have gotten the hang of skiing."

"There are exceptions," Espen said. "There are a few who can ski well."

"Phooey!" Haakon said. "They ski like Swedes! You can pretty well count on outrunning them. And even if they do catch up with you, they still have to be able to shoot straight to hit you. Can you imagine how hard it is to shoot after skiing hard? Plus, up here in the mountains, the light is funny. It bends things."

Espen knew that. A faraway mountain could look like a nearby boulder. A nearby stump could look like a faraway person.

"Do you always carry that?" Espen said, nodding at the pistol in Haakon's belt.

Haakon pulled his anorak down over the gun. "In case of emergency," he said.

"Doesn't it endanger you? Wouldn't it be a lot trickier pretending to be an innocent skier when you're carrying an illegal weapon?"

"Sometimes it's a good thing to have," Haakon replied, and he skied on.

Good to have to shoot at the Germans? Espen wondered, as he pushed off with his poles. *Or who?*

⤙—⤚

Espen had to force himself not to look behind him, even though he couldn't shake the feeling of being watched. Maybe it was the piercing glare of the moon, like a huge, all-seeing, all-knowing eye staring down at them. Finally, when the moon worked its way west, behind them, Espen took a moment to glance over his shoulder. There, silhouetted against its light, he saw something. A shape, a dark shape, moving along a ridge.

"Haakon," he said. "Look back."

Haakon stopped and turned. Squinted. Raised his binoculars to his eyes. "I guess there are a few of them," he said.

"A few!" Espen exclaimed.

"Looks like four of them—maybe a kilometer behind us."

"Are they . . . ?" Espen began.

"Chasing us?" Haakon finished. "I don't know what else they're doing out here in the middle of the night."

"Can they catch us?" Espen asked.

"No," Haakon said, slipping the straps of his poles over his mittens and pushing off. "Not if we don't make any mistakes."

⤙—⤚

Espen knew that he and Haakon couldn't ski endlessly without resting, especially not at this pace. But neither could their pursuers. Whoever could keep going the longest would win. The pursuers had an advantage, though. They would have tracks to follow, even after Espen and Haakon stopped. *If* they ever stopped.

"I have an idea," Haakon said between panting breaths.

Good, Espen thought, *because I don't.*

How long could they keep going? Espen wondered. It had been many hours since he had left Soria's farm, where he had hidden the previous night and all through the long day. Sometime during the day, Kari and Solveig had arrived, bringing him his skis, boots, and poles. Once inside, they emptied their pockets of ski wax and presented Espen with sandwiches and a thermos—and a plan. Things had been arranged, they said. He was going to Sweden.

"I'm not going anywhere until you tell me what happened at my house last night," Espen had said when they all were gathered around the table. *"How are my parents? Ingrid?"*

"Ingrid's a bit hoarse after the throttling they gave her—"

"Throttling!" Espen cried.

"—but as feisty as ever," Kari finished. *"Of course, she wouldn't say anything, and they had to give up."*

"Oh!" Solveig said suddenly, rummaging in her back-pack. "She gave me this to give to you." She handed Espen one of Ingrid's diaries. *1939*, it said on the spine.

"Why would she give me this?" Espen asked. He slid the book from its case, opened it, and immediately saw the money tucked between the pages—his escape money. He also saw that the entries were from recent days, not from 1939. "What about the others?"

"She said, 'They are buried in the cold, cold ground.' Except," Solveig added, "the diary labeled 1945. Apparently, the Gestapo took that one."

Espen smiled, realizing that his clever sister had switched the books in their cases. The Gestapo had taken the harmless diary from 1939, and he had gotten the incriminating one.

Solveig nodded at the book. "She said you should burn that one."

"No," Espen said. "I'll take it with me." He slid the diary into the back pocket of his rucksack. "And how are Mor and Far?"

"Your mother is fine. Your father . . ." Solveig paused.

"What?" Espen said, not wanting to hear the answer.

"He's been arrested. We think they're taking him to Grini."

Grini, the concentration camp near Oslo.

Espen closed his eyes against a kind of white pain that was pooling in his head.

"It's not the worst place the Nazis have to offer," Mr. Soria said.

"Not that it's any picnic," Kari added.

And with his bad ulcer . . . Espen thought. "I should—" he started to say.

"No, you should not." Solveig reached across the table; he felt her warm hand on his. "You know he wouldn't want you to come back on his account. And you know you—you just can't!"

⌐—#—◦

But, now, as he skied farther and farther from home, he felt the tug of invisible strings, pulling him back. Then he remembered the shadowy figures in pursuit and he knew there was no possibility of turning back. Solveig had been right. And Tante Marie had been right when she'd said it was possible to know too much.

Espen knew where radio transmissions occurred, where airdrops were made, and the locations of Milorg camps. He knew section heads, XU agents, and scores of people who played roles both large and small. He could read code and reveal invisible inks. Now he knew everything about the German compound, too.

No, there was no possibility of turning back, not even stopping for a moment. Not to remove a layer of sweaty clothing, not to clear off steamy glasses, and not to scrape the ice off the bottom of their skis. They simply had to press on and try to make Haakon's idea work.

The Lake

Below them lay what looked like a big patchwork quilt stitched together of scraps of gleaming black ice and bright patches of snow.

"There it is," Haakon said. "Head for the ice."

They plunged down the hill and onto the lake, steering for the black spots. The ice was slippery; it was hard to keep their skis under them. Weaving in between the snowy patches, making sure an errant ski or pole didn't leave a mark in the snow, made for slow going.

When the moon set behind the western mountains, the light faded, and their shadows dissolved. Haakon became a dim figure moving ahead of Espen. It would be hard for anyone to see them from a distance, Espen realized. Their scheme just might work.

"We should get off the lake and out of sight before the sun rises," Haakon said.

Ah, yes, the sun, Espen remembered. *That.*

"I think we've lost them, anyhow," Haakon added.

Espen doubted it, but he was too tired to disagree.

When they reached the edge of the lake, Haakon said,

"Now that we're on snow, plant your poles in front of you."

Espen did as he was told, punching the sharp points of his poles into the snow ahead of him at a slant. This was a clever strategy, too. It would, he realized, make it look as if they had been skiing *toward* and *onto* the lake instead of *off* and *away* from it.

They went along in this manner for some time until a dark shape appeared ahead of them: a small stone hut. Using the same backward pole plant, they continued to the hut. Mixed in among other, older tracks, theirs might be lost.

"Do you think it's safe to stop?" Espen asked as they stepped carefully out of their ski bindings. They picked up their skis and, walking backward, carried them into the hut.

"We have to sleep," Haakon said.

Sleep? Espen wondered. It seemed unlikely.

The Next Night

ometime during the day, while Espen dozed, his first guide left, and a second one arrived, then woke him to start their trek. The winter days were short, and his troubled slumber hadn't felt like enough rest to Espen. The tin of sardines, hard biscuits, and thermos of warm currant juice hadn't seemed like enough food, either. Nonetheless, just after twilight, he and his new guide set off.

It was so cold that the snow snapped, whined, and squeaked under their skis. If there had been an army of tanks following them, Espen doubted he could have heard it. All he could hear was the squeal and crunch of his skis and the steady *clickity-clack* of his poles breaking through the icy crust.

Even though they hadn't seen anyone, Espen still felt as if they were being followed, and he mentioned this to his new guide, who was also named Haakon. "We have no imagination when it comes to code names," the guide had explained.

Haakon II took out his binoculars and scanned the expanse of white. He turned this way and that, then shook his head. "Don't see anything," he said, and he offered the binoculars to Espen. "I think you lost them yesterday."

Espen did not think so. He felt as if he could see his pursuers in his mind's eye, like dark, menacing shadows. As the moon rose, his own shadow appeared alongside him, matching him stride for stride.

He kept his eyes on the tails of Haakon II's skis and for a while thought of nothing but going faster. But there had been little sleep and even less food, and he was tired. They skied on and on until he was so tired, he wondered if it was possible to sleep while skiing. Perhaps he dozed, for he began to feel at times that he was not skiing at all but swimming—at nightfall, the water and sky bruised purple, the cool water peeling away from him like petals from a rose. He swam through dark air into a liquid sky.

The air moved around him as if from the beating of large wings, and he felt something settle on his shoulder. *Munin,* he thought sleepily. *Memory has come to whisper in my ear.*

He thought of when he'd left Soria's farm—had it only been the previous night? After plans had been made, he and Solveig had waited out the daylight hours until evening fell. At last, they had stepped out of the bright kitchen into the cold darkness. Yet not dark, really. The moon was very bright, with only one edge gnawed away by a hungry sky.

Espen tossed his skis onto the snow and stared at them. Did he really have to go? Solveig held his poles for him just steps away. He could feel the warmth of her from where he was.

"It's bright tonight," she said.

"Ja," Espen agreed.

"Should make for good traveling," she added.

Espen looked out at the expanse of snow, glittering in the moonlight.

"It will be a lot of uphill," Solveig said.

Espen nodded, and they both looked for a moment at the rising hills and the distant mountain peaks glinting like knife blades.

"Take care," Solveig said.

Espen nodded again. Solveig was so calm and strong. He couldn't speak. He quickly stepped into the bindings of his skis and pulled the straps tight.

"I'll check on your family, Espen," Solveig said, "and somehow get word to you."

He thought he heard her voice quaver a little, but when he turned to her, she simply held out his poles. He took them, then tossed them down and pulled her to him in an embrace. If only . . . , *he thought.* If only I could hold her to me all the long way to Sweden.

"Your friends are back," Haakon II said.

"What?" Espen swam out of his memory and back to the cold, windswept plateau.

"Two of them, anyway," Haakon II added.

Espen glanced behind him and saw two figures, barely visible against the snow. There was not much in the landscape to shield Espen and his guide from view. Sometimes they were briefly separated by a hill, or once in a while a low, dark cloud would scud by, veiling the moon. Their pursuers were close enough, and the moon offered so much light that he could tell they were wearing the white camouflage suits of one of the mountain divisions. He and Haakon II didn't have that advantage; they had been trying to pass as civilians. Their dark clothing made them stand out like two black bull's-eyes on an all-white target.

Within Range

AKSEL

They were nearly within shooting distance now, Aksel thought. It had taken longer than he'd hoped to catch up with them. The two Germans who had started out with them had dropped out of the chase sometime the previous night and had not been seen since.

Aksel and Kjell had argued about which direction the tracks led and had wasted a lot of time on that lake. They were hungry and tired, so they had stopped, eaten some sandwiches, and slept for a few hours. By some lucky break, they came upon the trail again. And they had done well. They had begun to close the gap.

"I think I could hit him," Aksel said. He stopped and raised his binoculars, eyeing the two dots moving on the snow in the distance. From his perch on the top of a hill, Aksel observed their progress for a moment—there was one small hill separating them, but the skiers would soon move out of its shadow.

"You think you can, but you won't," Kjell said. "For one thing, they must be at least a half kilometer away." He took the binoculars and glanced through them. "For another, they're moving. Plus, you're tired. Look at you—you're dripping sweat. You'll have sweat in your eyes. Your muscles are fatigued; you won't be steady. It'll be a lot harder to shoot straight than you think."

"If I miss, so what?" Aksel said. "It'll be worth it to make them nervous."

"The amount of time you take to shoot will make you lose more ground than it's worth," Kjell said. "It's better to keep skiing and gain on them."

Kjell skied on, but Aksel stayed where he was. He watched Kjell moving ahead of him, the gap between them widening. If Espen and the others maintained this pace, Aksel didn't think he'd be able to keep up much longer. He might never get another chance as good as this one.

Aksel dropped his poles and slipped the rifle from his back. He was in a good position. Kjell had moved on ahead but wasn't in the line of fire. Aksel raised the rifle to his shoulder, pulled back the bolt, let his breath out in a long, slow exhale, took aim, and pulled the trigger.

Espen heard the distant crack of the gun and the high *zing* of a bullet. Ahead of him, Haakon II cursed a blue streak.

"Keep moving!" the guide shouted. "It's harder to hit a moving target."

Espen had no intention of stopping—he sprinted. He heard another crack and the *ping* of a bullet hitting rock, and then another crack. Should he swerve? Move an inch to the left or to the right? Duck? While he wondered, two or possibly three more shots were fired, and then he felt the impact, felt himself being lifted off his feet and pitching forward—as if someone had given him a shove from behind. He thought, *If I can just keep my footing . . . if I can just keep on skiing . . .* but he felt the wind whistling past his ears and saw the ground rushing up toward him . . .

Aksel had five rounds and was just getting the fourth shot off when he saw Kjell skiing back toward him. He tried to get one more shot off, but Kjell reached him before he had a chance and wrested the rifle out of his hands.

"You stupid ass!" Kjell said. "You could kill him!"

"That's the point, isn't it?" Aksel said. "He's a criminal."

"That would be about the stupidest thing you've ever done," Kjell said, "and you've done a lot of them."

"You may have become accustomed to speaking to me in those terms back in our school days," Aksel said, "but may I remind you that you are my subordinate—"

"Listen to me, you idiot. Do you realize that his guide is probably carrying a revolver?"

"So what? He can't hit us with that thing at this distance."

"It isn't for shooting *us*. It's for shooting Espen."

"What?" Aksel said. "Why?"

"Good grief, you're thick," Kjell said. "Better dead than captured, that's why. Do you have any idea how much information Espen has? How many people he knows? XU can't risk him being taken alive. Listen, Aksel, I don't even know why I'm bothering to explain this to you, but if you want to make your superiors angry—*again*—go ahead, shoot Espen. But if you intend to impress anyone, you have to bring him back alive. Maybe then you could rectify your whole sorry situation back in Lilleby."

Aksel shot him a dirty look.

"But you know what?" Kjell went on. "That's never going to happen. You're never going to get him. Why? Because you're too bloody slow. You're not a good enough skier to catch up to him. Maybe I could catch him—without you along—but you—"

"Why are you telling me this *now?*" Aksel gestured out at the distant scene, where Espen lay sprawled in the snow. "I hit him. He's dead."

Snow

It had started to snow, in earnest this time, like a heavy dusting of powdered sugar that collected rapidly on Aksel's skis and clothing and obscured his vision, especially as he and Kjell sped down the hill. It was inconvenient, Aksel thought, but nothing that would prevent them from finding a body lying out in the open.

At the foot of the slope, there was still one smaller hill to go. Aksel tried to work through the possibilities as he started up the hill. Perhaps Espen was only wounded, and they could still bring him back with them, alive. Espen's guide, Aksel supposed, would be long gone. Of course, the guide might have finished Espen off before he could be reached. The snow had been so loud a little earlier that Aksel might not have heard the gunshot. Now, though, enough snow had fallen that it was like skiing on butter—smooth and quiet—so quiet, he could hear the tiny flakes tapping against his anorak. One way or another, Aksel had to assume Espen was dead, and he was, he had to admit, relieved that the chase was over. Of course, there would be the body to deal with, Aksel thought.

But as he crested the hill, he looked down and saw that there wasn't a body.

There was nothing. No body. No guide. No blood, even. Kjell stood at the bottom of the hill, where the body should have been, surveying the scene.

"Maybe it wasn't here," Aksel said when he reached Kjell. "Maybe it was a little farther along—over the next rise."

Kjell shook his head. "No," he said, "it was here." He laughed.

"I don't see what's so funny," Aksel said.

"You wouldn't," Kjell said, still laughing.

Aksel didn't feel like laughing. In frustration, he fired his gun into the air. This made Kjell hoot with laughter.

"Now what?" Aksel asked.

"That was your last shot!" Kjell said. "You're out of ammunition."

A Joke About Chickens

L ying facedown in the snow, Espen thought of a joke he had forgotten to tell his sister. A farmer, so the joke went, had gotten a threatening letter from the occupying regime about his inability to keep them supplied with enough eggs. The farmer sent this reply: *Have submitted your document to the individuals concerned (the hens), but inasmuch as they refused to comply, they have been court-martialed, placed before a firing squad, and executed.*

Now he knew how the chickens felt.

"Can you get up? Can you move?"

Espen turned his head to see Haakon II standing over him. "What just happened?" he asked, getting to his knees.

Haakon II helped him to his feet. "Never mind. Can you ski?"

Yes, Espen thought he could ski, and they started off, with him once again following in Haakon II's tracks.

Haakon II glanced back at Espen. "You're OK?" he said.

Espen nodded. He'd been hit; he'd felt it, yet he was skiing now. He felt fine. He didn't feel any pain. He wasn't dead—or maybe, it occurred to him, he just wasn't dead *yet*.

There must be a hole in him somewhere. And if there was a hole in him, he must be bleeding. He would have liked to check himself for bullet holes, but he knew they had to move as fast as they could, *away*.

He felt strangely energized, as if he hadn't been skiing as hard as he could for hours on end. As if he hadn't been hit by a bullet. Things were good now: the moon had disappeared behind dark clouds, and snow flew around them, thick and fast, the flakes as big as handkerchiefs. It would be too bad to let their pursuers catch up now, just when they had a decent chance of losing them. And it really would be too bad to be dying, Espen thought. The skiing was so *good,* and he felt like he could go on forever. And it was quiet. So quiet, he could hear the world breathing, in and out, in and out. Or perhaps that was just the sound of his skis whispering against the snow.

The Checkpoint

You're a lucky fellow," said Espen's third guide—
also named Haakon—after hearing about his
brush with death. Espen and his previous guide,
Haakon II, had spent most of the day "sleeping" in a snowbank. After establishing that
Espen was not bleeding anywhere, they had climbed into
their sleeping bags and let the snow drift over them. At
some point, Haakon II had gone away and Haakon III had
arrived.

"*Ja,* you're a lucky one," his new guide commented,
skiing alongside him.

"I suppose I am," Espen said.

"Still feeling lucky?" Haakon III said.

"Why?" Espen asked.

"Up ahead you will have to cross a road—the road that
goes over the pass—and there is a control point thoro,"
Haakon III said.

"What?"

"A control point," Haakon III repeated. "A checkpoint.
Two Germans were shot around here somewhere, and the
Gestapo have set up a roadblock."

"I can't go through a checkpoint!" Espen said. "That'll be the end of me. Can't we avoid it?"

"Did you bring mountain climbing equipment with you?"

"No." Espen looked at the steep mountain peaks that rose on either side of the trail that led through the pass. "What about going around?" he asked hopefully.

"How about adding another twenty-four hours to your trip?" Haakon III said. "Without a guide, and"—he nodded at the sky behind them, churning with dark clouds—"with a storm brewing."

"Well, I can't go through a checkpoint!" Espen said.

"You don't have fake identification papers?"

"No, I only have a real ID with a fake medical exemption."

Haakon III squinted at Espen and pulled at the icicles that clung to his beard. "You and I," he said, "we're quite alike, don't you think?"

"No, not really," Espen replied.

"Yes, I think so," Haakon III insisted. "Do you have a good memory?"

"Nothing wrong with it," Espen said, irritated at the guide's sidetracks.

"Look at this now." Haakon III pulled out his ID and showed it to Espen. "That's me, clean-shaven." He pointed to the photo, which was wrinkled, creased, and dirty. If he squinted at it just so, Espen supposed they could be mistaken for each other.

"I can't take your ID!" Espen said. "What will you use?"

"Oof!" Haakon III exclaimed. "I've got a dozen of them! So, now pay attention. You will have to learn my parents' names and birthdays and also my grandparents' names and birthdays. Those Germans will ask you about all of them, and if there is the slightest discrepancy"—he paused for a moment to wipe his nose with the back of his sleeve—"it's straight into an interrogation room with you. Do you understand?" He drilled Espen on his "relatives" and then said, "OK, I leave you here, and on the other side of the checkpoint, you'll meet your next guide."

Espen took Haakon III's identification card and said good-bye. Then he skied on alone, trying to transform himself into Jens Christiansen, lumberman, whose parents were Arne Jakob Christiansen and Ruth Ragnhild, whose birthdays were June 11, 1899, and November 17, 1900.

The rhythm of his skiing became the rhythm of the names of his "parents" and "grandparents," their birthdays and ages. *Kick and glide, kick and glide.*

"Arne Jakob Christiansen" (*kick*) " born June 11" (*glide*) "1899, father," Espen recited. His poles punctuated his poetry with their *chick-chocking.* "Ruth Ragnhild" (*chick*) "born November 17, 1900" (*chock*) "mother. Johan Trygve Christiansen" (*kick*) "born April 12, 1862" (*glide*) "grandfather" (*chick*) . . .

As he approached the checkpoint, Espen took a look over his shoulder. He hadn't seen his pursuers since before they'd fired at him, but he still felt their presence.

The patrol came out of his shelter. "Your skis, *bitte*," he said. "Take them off."

Espen slipped out of his bindings and dropped his poles onto the snow.

He imagined the distant skiers behind him growing closer and larger and more real. At the same time, he had to concentrate on the questions and on providing the right answers. He answered the first few questions correctly and then lost his concentration and said, "Johan Trygve Christiansen."

"Is your grandmother?" the patrol asked.

"Ha-ha!" Espen tried to laugh. "No, of course not. That's my grandfather. My grandmother is . . ." Espen's mind raced through his list—now it was all out of order and jumbled in his brain.

"Your grandmother?" the patrol prompted him again.

The names had fled. Without the rhythm of the skiing, the words didn't come back to him.

The patrol shifted his weight, lifting one foot, then the other; he shook his arms and hands as if to get the blood flowing. He was cold; Espen could see that he didn't want to stand outside any longer than necessary.

"Here's something funny about my grandmother," Espen said. "My grandmother started skiing ten kilometers a day when she was sixty."

"Uh-huh," the patrol said.

"She's ninety-five today," Espen said, "and we don't know where the devil she is!"

The patrol didn't laugh.

"See, it's a joke," Espen said. He started to explain it, but the soldier just said, "Fine," and handed the paper back.

Espen took one glance behind him before leaping back onto his skis. Nothing. He cinched his bindings tightly to his boots, pushed off with his poles, and headed east to meet his next guide.

The Fourth Night

ow, by Espen's reckoning, it was the fourth night. He was traveling with Haakon IV. The snow whipped about them in gusts and stung his face like clouds of angry wasps.

He curled his hands into fists inside his mittens to try to warm his numb fingers. The wind sliced through every layer of his wool clothing, mincing his flesh and piercing his very core. He closed his eyes against it and tried to imagine warmth. He tried to call back the feeling of Solveig's warm arms encircling him as they'd stood together outside the Soria farm. Tried to conjure back the warmth of that kitchen, the fragrance of the food, the sight of Solveig's face, bright as sunlight . . .

"I'll be here when you get back," she'd said. "I won't forget you."

How long would he be gone? Would Munin find him wherever he went, to bring him memories of her, of Ingrid and his parents?

"I fear for Thought, yet more anxious am I for Memory," Odin had said.

Would he remember these years? He felt he would

never—*could* never—forget this time under the Nazi fist, but he wasn't sure. Would it be better to forget?

The wind kicked up the snow in smokelike swirls of white that blotted out the landmarks, the trail ahead, and, often, his guide. Sometimes Espen glimpsed the tails of Haakon IV's skis; other times just his guide's upper body appeared to float above the swirling snow. But more and more, Haakon IV was becoming more invisible than visible. Even his tracks were filling in with snow.

Our tracks, Espen realized, *are filling in with snow!*

There was a lull in the wind, and Espen glanced back. Did he only imagine that he saw someone moving behind him? If there really was someone, he could not call up any anger—not even fear, really. It was as if this was just the way it had to be, and all he felt was admiration for his pursuer's elegant stride.

Sometime in the night, wind and snow and darkness all became one thing and the only thing. He would suddenly feel himself plunging down a hill or hurtling around a curve, but sometimes he could not tell if he was skiing on snow or sky. Was he skiing at all or adrift on an ocean of air?

He stopped and tried to look around, but it was as if the world had disappeared. There were no mountains, no trees, no sky. The wind seemed to have swept away the very ground. He cleaned the ice and snow off his glasses, but it made no difference. Now even Haakon IV was gone, swallowed by blowing snow. Espen tried to listen for a voice, or anything, but all he could hear was the thrashing wind.

He made out a dark shape nearby—a large boulder—and he moved over to it, took off his skis, and crouched behind it. Maybe the wind would let up, and he could find his guide again. He would just close his eyes for a moment—he wouldn't let himself sleep. He knew the danger of that. No, he would just close his eyes against the stinging snow.

The Draug

E spen felt a presence, and he opened his eyes, expecting to see Haakon IV next to him. But it was not Haakon.

"Kjell?" he shouted into the wind. "What are you doing here?"

"Hiding behind this rock. Same as you," Kjell shouted back.

"Did you shoot at me?" Espen said. "I'd punch you in the face right now if I had enough energy."

"That was Aksel," Kjell said. "What happened, anyway? You ski devilishly well for someone with a bullet in him."

Espen reached for his rucksack. "I used to complain that Ingrid's writing habit was endangering our whole family, but it turns out . . ." He dug around and pulled out Ingrid's diary and then showed Kjell the hole bored into the leather case and nearly through the entire book. "It turns out, her diary saved my life."

Kjell took the book from him and turned it over in his hands. He shook his head. "I think even Aksel was surprised that he hit you. It's a good thing he was so far away, or . . ."

"Where *is* Aksel?" Espen said. "If he were here, we'd have a real party."

"*Ja.*" Kjell laughed. "Too bad he couldn't come. He got mad, shot off all his ammunition, and went home."

"Ha," Espen said. "So, how about something to eat?"

"Thank you." Kjell looked at Espen expectantly, then finally asked, "Well, what do you have?"

"I was hoping *you* had something," Espen said.

Kjell shook his head.

Espen contemplated his empty belly for a few moments. "You didn't go home with Aksel," he said.

"Seems there's a holdup with *Bestemor's* medicine. Aksel says he can remedy that just as soon as I get back to Lilleby—with you."

"I see," Espen said.

Kjell dug into his waistband and pulled out a revolver. "Uncomfortable," he said, slipping the gun into his jacket pocket.

"Very," Espen agreed.

The wind gusted suddenly and sent a blast of icy crystals at their faces.

"I don't want to have to take you back," Kjell told him.

"I don't particularly want to go," Espen replied.

There was a period of thrashing wind, and they were silent. Finally, Kjell said, "You haven't anything in a thermos, even?"

Espen noticed now that Kjell's lips were cracked and

swollen. There was dried blood on his chin and anorak from where they had bled. He pulled his thermos from his rucksack and poured the last bit of juice into the cup and handed it to Kjell.

Espen watched Kjell tip the cup and drain the last bit of liquid, and thought of Tante Marie telling him about Odin drinking from the well of wisdom. When Odin drank, she'd said, the future was revealed to him. Odin saw all the sorrow and despair that would befall the human race, and he saw how people could bear and even conquer the evil that brought grief and desolation to the world. How? Espen wondered now. He wished he could remember how it was that humankind could overcome all this.

He also wished that he could see the future, so that he could know what would be the right thing to do. If he went back with Kjell, maybe he could get his father out of prison. Maybe he could save his mother and Ingrid from any further retaliation. He could help Kjell's grandmother and, of course, Kjell.

In a sudden burst of memory, Espen recalled that he had once vowed to save Kjell from the Nazis. But had he ever even tried? Here was his chance to do it, to really save him. He could save Kjell from whatever punishment Aksel or the Gestapo might have in store for him if he returned without Espen. Clearly, he could help a lot of people by going back. Perhaps that was the right thing to do.

Espen knew he would be arrested, and the Gestapo

would torture him. Although he would never intend to, he might give away the names of others. Many others. Of course he should not go back.

At some point, this storm was going to let up. Espen wondered, in a kind of distant, unemotional way, what would happen then. The issue of whether he would return with Kjell or not might be decided for them, he thought, if they were both frozen stiff by morning.

Which seemed possible. The wind howled, and the cold turned even more savage, taking huge, wolflike bites at their flesh. They pulled their hoods tighter, tucked their heads and stayed crouched behind the rock so long, it seemed as if all the seasons might have passed by. Spring might have come and gone and summer arrived.

Behind his closed eyes, the image of the *draug* appeared, just as it had that summer day when he and Kjell and Ingrid had been out on the fjord in the rowboat.

The sun had settled in the sky between two mountain peaks and shone down on them, infusing everything with a beautiful, golden tone.

Espen was teasing Ingrid about a draug *coming up and snatching her right out of the boat.*

"Look, though," Kjell said. He was leaning over the boat, gazing into the black water. "There is a draug."

Espen looked past his reflection into the darkness.

Somewhere, far below the surface, a thing began to take shape, a huge gray beast, slowly swimming around and around below them, its great bulging eyes staring up at them.

Had he seen a *draug* that day? Had it been real? And *now,* was *Kjell* really real, or was he only imagining him?

Before Espen opened his eyes, the *draug* disappeared with a flip of its tail, leaving only a bright flickering on the surface of the water. And suddenly, Espen thought of how he could save Kjell—*really* save him. Not just from retribution when he returned home but from the wrath of the whole country once the war was over.

"Why don't you come to Sweden with me?" he asked.

Kjell shook his head. "*Bestemor . . . ,*" he said.

"Don't worry about your grandmother," Espen told him. "I have connections. I can make sure she gets the care she needs. Really, Kjell. Just come with me. You can . . . start over."

"No," Kjell said. "I chose my path; I'll stick to it."

"Why, Kjell?" Espen asked. "Why did you join them, anyway?"

"My *bestemor*—"

"No." Espen stopped him. "Why did you, *really?*"

"I wanted to put the world right."

Espen's head jerked up, and he stared at Kjell. "That's what *I* wanted to do," he said.

"See?" Kjell said. "We're not so different, you and I."

Weren't they? Espen wondered. He remembered thinking that Kjell had caught a troll splinter in his eye, making everything right seem wrong, everything wrong seem right.

Who was right? And what was the right thing to do? If only the wind would let up, Espen thought, so he could *think*.

All he knew, as the storm raged around them, tore at their clothing, rattled their bones, and scoured their faces raw, was that he had been on a journey. He was still on a journey; he had set himself on this path, and he couldn't turn back now because the going was difficult or because the stakes were high or for any reason at all. He believed in what he was doing, even if it was only a small thing. A tiny part of the whole effort was still a part—maybe even a key part. Who could know until it was all over? And the important thing was to do what you believed in your heart to be the right thing—no, not *believed*, what you *knew* to be the right thing.

His father had said once that people could become snow-blind to what was just basic human decency, but behind that temporary blindness, they could see; they knew perfectly well what was the right thing to do.

Espen was not going to be one of those people. He was going to *watch with both eyes*. He should probably be watching Kjell with both eyes *right now*, since Kjell had a gun and he did not, but he could not keep his eyes open against the needle-sharp snow. He could not keep his head up, could no longer speak, could, in fact, barely think.

They hunkered down, shielding their heads and faces with their arms. Kjell's hood had blown back, and Espen pulled it up for him, then left his arm covering his old friend's head.

When the storm at last abated, Espen lifted his head, and Kjell was gone. Espen's arm rested on the rock. The space where Kjell had been had filled in with snow. There were no ski tracks to mark which way he'd gone, but there wouldn't be. The wind had scoured and polished the world, so the whole of it gleamed, shiny and fragile as a china plate.

Sweden

Heading east, Espen squinted against the bright sun. A short time later, he found his guide sitting on the lee side of the mountain behind a pile of rocks.

"Where have you been?" Haakon IV asked.

"I checked into the Ritz," Espen said.

Haakon IV grunted. "Hope you had a lovely stay."

The two of them skied together for a while before meeting with Espen's fifth and final guide. Espen and Haakon V traveled mostly downhill, it seemed, and were soon among the trees. A damp fog swirled around them, becoming thicker and thicker as they went on, until finally it obscured even the nearest tree trunks. Still, Haakon V strode confidently forward.

"Not long now," he said. "Almost there."

Espen ached with the desire to *be* there, to be done skiing, to stop. But it felt like a long time went by. A very long time. And in the meantime, the fog grew thicker.

"Now," Haakon V said, "you can almost smell it."

Espen could not smell anything, and when they came upon a double set of ski tracks, he began to suspect they had been skiing in circles. Finally, he asked, "Are we lost?"

"How should I know?" Haakon V threw up his hands. "I've no idea where we are, so I can't say whether we're lost or not! We should be almost to Sweden. Or we could have been in Sweden already and are now back in Norway."

"Are we at least going in the right direction?" Espen asked.

Haakon V scratched his beard and peered off into the fog. "How can anyone tell?" he said finally.

"Haven't you got a compass?"

Haakon V admitted that he didn't.

"Why didn't you tell me you didn't have one?" Espen slipped off his rucksack and produced the compass Tante Marie had given him.

Haakon V looked down at it. He pursed his lips as if giving it serious consideration. At last he handed it back and admitted he didn't know how to use it.

Espen showed him how to take a bearing, and they skied on, headed, Espen knew for sure, *east.*

Not long after, Espen began to smell something. Sweden? he wondered. It smelled like wood smoke. Soon a cabin loomed out of the fog.

"Ha!" said Haakon V. "Looks like Hjalmar's place. That compass you got there? That works real swell. We'll be safe and snug here tonight. Just a short walk to Sweden in the morning."

Hjalmar was a big, gentle man with large hands that

seemed to gather them in. Those hands had gathered plenty of other people in, too. And dogs. He gave the two travelers space on the floor near the fireplace while he, his wife, his grandfather, several children, and three dogs squeezed into the other room and, apparently, the one bed in it.

Curled up in his sleeping bag, gazing into the gently crackling fire, Espen tried to stay awake to savor the feeling of being dry, warm, and almost in Sweden. He tried to stay awake long enough to say a prayer for his family, for Solveig, and for those whose work went on in Norway. But somewhere in the midst of Haakon V's snoring, the snapping and popping of the fire, the groans of the dogs as they were pushed aside by little feet in the next room, and the sighing and breathing of a houseful of people, he fell fast asleep.

They were all up the next morning before the sun rose. Haakon V waved good-bye and skied back to wherever he had come from, one compass richer, and Espen, at Hjalmar's request, left his skis in the barn.

Without his skis, without a guide, and without even a compass, Espen felt light, almost weightless, as he walked on alone.

At the top of a hill, he emerged from the forest as the sun peeped up over the horizon. From this place, he could look back at the broad sweep of Norway. The sun was just rising, and the light struck the snow-covered mountain peaks, making them glint and gleam like jeweled turbans. Below, the valleys were still shrouded in darkness.

In one of those dark valleys, he had left his family, his friends, and Solveig. Back there somewhere was his childhood. *That* was something he would never see again. Who was he now? he wondered. Would he walk out of Norway and into the man he would become?

For a few moments, Espen watched as the light crept down the mountainsides, illuminating the forests. He ached with loneliness already, an ache as deep and dark as those valleys, yet he felt a kind of shimmering joy, too, bright as the far peaks he was leaving behind, bright as the sunshine he turned toward.

Author's Note

T he historical events in this story are true: The refusal of parents, students, and teachers to join Nazi organizations or sign oaths of allegiance to the Nazi Party; the letter read by the clergy and their subsequent resignations; the arrests of 1,300 teachers all over Norway; the beatings, torture, and executions; the prohibition of scouting and the confiscation of radios and many other items; the rationing of almost everything; the extreme hunger; the death penalty for radio listening or for possessing anti-German literature; the compulsory Labor Service and the attempt to force young men and women into it by withholding their ration cards; and the 760 Norwegian Jews sent to Auschwitz. All these things really happened.

With the exception of major historical figures, the characters in this story are fictional, including Espen. The town of Lilleby and the fjord on which it is situated are also fictional. However, many of Espen's experiences are based on the real-life experiences of Erling Storrusten, who was a teenager in the town of Lillehammer in central Norway during the years of the Occupation, 1940–1945.

Like the fictional Espen, the real Erling Storrusten got his start in the Resistance by delivering underground newspapers. He then became a courier, transporting documents by bicycle or on skis. As a courier, he (as a test) retrieved a revolver from a cabin near a large encampment of Germans and delivered letters by train and ski (without official travel permits) to the clergy and Milorg units up and down the Gudbrandsdalen Valley. He also made many trips to a fox farm on his bicycle or on skis. One night, he stopped to watch a group of capercaillies (black grouse) tranquilly pecking gravel by the side of the road, a reminder of peace in the turmoil of the war years.

When his section head died, Erling had to take over the job himself. When the Labor Service was instituted, he was given a diagnosis of consumption (tuberculosis) by a sympathetic doctor so he could continue his work. Eventually, he became a spy for XU, the intelligence branch of the Resistance, and he did, indeed, make a detailed map of the German headquarters for the 360,000 soldiers in *Festung Norwegen* (Fortress Norway). Erling accomplished this by following what he called "the Gudbrandsdal Method," or the simplest way: pretending to trade potatoes for trinkets with the starving prisoners of war.

He and his girlfriend, Aase-Berit (whose family's home he stayed in to avoid capture) sometimes went on missions together, during which she served as a kind of "camouflage" for him. She also helped the Red Cross feed refugees from northern Norway.

The events in the chapter entitled "'It's Full of Gestapo in There'" occurred in a similar way for Erling. One evening, while he was delivering "the post," three Gestapo officers rushed toward him—and then past him—as he wheeled his bike to the street. (The cake box episode, however, is fiction.) Later, Erling's family was held hostage by the Gestapo, and his sister, Inger, was choked by one of them, who demanded to know where Erling was hiding. (He was at Aase-Berit's house.) Their neighbor Kiri and her boyfriend were taking wash off the line when they heard Inger screaming; they went to warn Erling, who left immediately—events unfolding in ways somewhat parallel to those in Espen's story. Earlier, Erling's father had told him, "If I should be taken hostage for you, the worst thing you could do for me is to come out of hiding to get me free." He was indeed taken as a hostage and imprisoned at Grini, a concentration camp near Oslo, where he underwent primitive stomach surgery for an ulcer by a fellow inmate. He survived the ordeal and returned home after the war.

After someone revealed his name, Erling escaped to neutral Sweden on skis, traveling at night to avoid detection. The journey took him five days, with five different guides. Erling and one of the guides used the ruse of planting their ski poles in such a way as to make it look as if they had been skiing in the opposite direction. Erling also had to use one

guide's identification card to get through a checkpoint—
which required him to learn the names and birthdays of the
guide's closest relatives, should he be interrogated. When
another of his guides got lost in the fog, Erling gave him his
own compass, after teaching him how to use it. Years later,
one of his guides confessed that he had been given orders to
shoot Erling if they were threatened with capture, because
Erling *knew too much!*

From Sweden, Erling made his way to England. He
agreed to parachute back into Norway as a spy, but the war
came to an end before he had the chance. He made it back to
Oslo in time for the celebration of freedom on June 6, 1945.
In Oslo, he bumped into Kiri. Perhaps they each enjoyed a
big piece of cake, with real whipped cream!

After the war, Erling and Aase-Berit were married. As a
boy, Erling had spent a lot of time on bicycles and skis, so
perhaps it was not surprising that he went into the trans-
portation industry, working in civil aviation (SAS) and,
later, as the director of the Norwegian Automobile Feder-
ation (NAF). He also wrote two popular books, *The Most
Beautiful Sea Voyage*, about the coastal trip from Bergen to
Kirkenes, and *The NAF Road Book*. The Storrustens traveled a lot, but when they lived in Norway, Aase-Berit taught
high school. Today they are retired and live near Oslo. They
have two children, seven grandchildren, and one great-
grandchild.

The experiences of other characters in the story are

based on those of real people. The exploits of Aksel Pedersen are based on those of a schoolmate of Erling's friends
who became a Gestapo man. The events in the chapter "The
Bicycle" are also based on real events.

My interest in this period in history was sparked by my
father's stories of relatives and friends who got involved in
Resistance efforts in Norway, including a doctor who per-
formed "emergency appendectomies" or wrapped faces in
gauze ("burn victims") for those who needed to disappear
for a while. Although the character of Kjell is fictional, the
idea of friends at odds was inspired by my father's close
friendship with someone who later became an official in the
Norwegian Nazi government during the Occupation.

Many Norwegian soccer or sports teams, when they
were usurped by the Nazis, reorganized into underground
teams, and some became Milorg groups. Although the
soccer team and Espen's friends and soccer mates Leif,
Ole, Stein, Per, and Gust are fictional, many similar experiences happened to men in Erling's circle. The chapter in
which the bicycle shop employee climbs through a window
to warn Ole, and then Ole warns Leif and Leif climbs into
an air shaft to escape the Gestapo, is based on real experiences of the men Erling worked with in Milorg. Erling and
his friends built a weapons depot ("Oleanna" in Espen's
story), which is where the real-life Snekkeren (the joiner)
worked as a radio operator. Once, while transporting a
radio part of Snekkeren's for repair, Erling was caught out

in the open by a German surveillance plane flying so low that he could see the pilot's face. Erling waved and shouted like an excited kid. The pilot waved back and flew away.

You can read more about Erling Storrusten ("The Potato Spy"), as well as many other fascinating stories, at Geoff and Else Ward's excellent website, www.wwiinorge.com.

Bonus for Code Breakers

rling's first spy mission was to identify several very large things being carried on flatbed train cars. These things were covered by tarps, and the train carrying them was heavily guarded by armed German soldiers. Erling bought a ticket and pretended to be a passenger unable to find the passenger car so that he could walk the length of the train and try to inspect what was under the tarps. When he figured out what was being transported, he sent a coded message to a contact up the rail line. The message was successfully delivered . . . and the items in question never made it to their destination.

The code might have looked something like this:

121415164793642312143523832577892542899913794661

Here's how this particular (simpler) code works:

1. The code is organized in groups of three numbers. Each group of three numbers equals one letter. The first number indicates the line on the page. The second number indicates the word in that line, and the third number indicates the letter in the word.

2. The code relies on having an agreed upon code book. In this case, the code book will be *Shadow on the Mountain*

3. The page number is hidden in the long line of numbers, above. (The 3 digit page number follows the first 6 *letters* in the coded message.)

Can you decipher the code and figure out what the message says? Once you've deciphered it, turn to page 273 to see if you have the correct answer.

For more codes and information about Erling's code, visit www.margipreus.com.

How to Make Your Own Invisible Ink

One of the invisible inks used by the Norwegian Resistance was developed by analyzing (in the laboratory of a veterinary school) the properties of an ink used by the Germans. The Norwegians then developed a different one by reversing the process. This ink was used successfully throughout the Occupation.

But invisible inks don't have to be complicated. There are also easy ways of making ink using simple ingredients found in your kitchen.

LEMON JUICE

To the juice of half a lemon add ½ teaspoon of water. Stir well.

Dip a cotton swab, a small paintbrush, or a toothpick into the solution and write a message on a piece of clean paper.

Allow the paper to air-dry.

Reveal the message by holding the paper over a heat source, such as a 100-watt lightbulb (*over* it, not on it). Don't leave the paper unattended.

Tip: For extra confusion, first write a decoy message

in pencil or pen. Then write your *real* secret message with your invisible ink between the lines.

Vinegar, apple juice, baking soda, sugar, or salt (mixed with a small amount of water) will also make an invisible ink that can be revealed with the heat sources mentioned above. Words written in vinegar can also be revealed with red cabbage juice.

MESSAGE IN CODE ANSWER

The code on page 270 spells out the following message:

ONE MAN TORPEDOES

This refers to small single-manned, torpedo-equipped submarines, also known as midget submarines or human torpedoes.

ERLING STORRUSTEN,
the Real "Espen,"
AND HIS
World of Espionage

Aase-Berit Grindal; her brother, Alv Magnus; and Erling
Storrusten lounge in the garden. (1943)

Lillehammer Tourist Hotel. The hotel and the surrounding forests were the headquarters of the Germans in Norway after they retreated from Finland in 1944. (ca. 1940s) (COURTESY OF ELSE WARD)

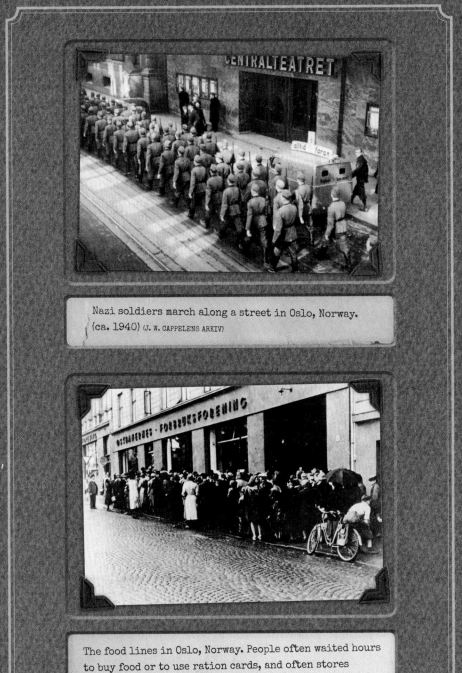

Nazi soldiers march along a street in Oslo, Norway.
(ca. 1940) (J. W. CAPPELENS ARKIV)

The food lines in Oslo, Norway. People often waited hours
to buy food or to use ration cards, and often stores
would sell out well before the crowds disappeared.
(1942) (COLLECTION OF LIBRARY OF CONGRESS)

NORDMENN

KJEMP FOR NORGE

i Stortings_ta 12·OSLO

Nordmenn — Kjemp for Norge ("Nordic men — Fight for Norway"). A German Waffen SS propaganda poster that plays on the Norwegian ancestral heritage of the noble Vikings. The Waffen SS was a multinational, multiethnic military force of the Third Reich. (1942)
(ARTIST: HARALD DAMSLETH)

Bli med oss nordover! Den Norske Skijegerbataljon
("Follow us north! The Norwegian Ski Ranger Battalion").
A Norwegian Waffen SS propaganda poster. The white suit
was camouflage against the snow. Exposed areas such as
the face were smeared with "black fat" to prevent
frostbite. The Norwegian Waffen SS consisted primarily
of Norwegian citizens who willingly fought for the
Nazis. (1942) (ARTIST: HARALD DAMSLETH)

Erling Storrusten (left) and King Olav of Norway (right), at the 50th anniversary celebration of the end of the war. Erling's first guide, Taraldstad, told the king that when he escorted Erling to Sweden, he was given orders to shoot Erling if they were captured by the Germans! Erling knew too much about the Resistance to allow him to be interrogated by the Nazis. (1995)

Erling Storrusten stands outside a German bunker near the Lillehammer Tourist Hotel. (2007) (COURTESY OF ELSE WARD)

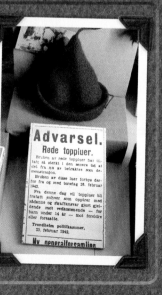

Advarsel.
Røde toppluer.

Bruken av røde toppluer har til-
tatt så sterkt i den senere tid at
det fra nu av betraktes som de-
monstrasjon.

Bruken av disse luer forbys der-
for fra og med torsdag 26. februar
1942.

Fra denne dag vil toppluer bli
fratatt enhver som opptrer med
sådanne og straffeansvar gjort gjel-
dende mot vedkommende — for
barn under 14 år — mot foreldre
eller foresatte.

Trondheim politikammer,
23. februar 1942.

Ny generalforsamling

Advarsel. Røde toppluer ("Warning. Red caps"), reads this exhibition card at the Norsk Hjemmefrontmuseum (Norway's Resistance Museum) in Olso, Norway. So many people wore the red caps in protest against the German occupation that the occupying power made it a punishable offense. The sign is a warning that the wearing of red hats would be banned beginning February 26, 1942.

(COURTESY OF ALEXANDER NILSSEN)

Margi Preus (left) with
Erling Storrusten and his
wife, Aase-Berit. (2011)

Timeline, 1940–1945

ere is a timeline of actual events that occurred during the Occupation of Norway by German forces. Efforts were made to coordinate the novel's events with the accurate historical dates wherever possible; however, for the purposes of narration and plot, some events in the story do not align exactly with historical dates.

1940

APRIL 9   Nazi Germany invades Norway

JUNE 7   King Haakon and government leave Norway for England

JUNE 9   Norwegian forces capitulate; the king and government decide to continue the fight from England

AUGUST 15   Children return to school for the first time since April 8

SEPTEMBER 25 Norwegian constitution abolished by Reichskommissar Terboven; all weapons to be turned over to the Germans by October 4

1941

FEBRUARY 17	Two-day strike by high school students against Nazi propaganda and bullying tactics of Quisling's *hird*
MARCH 4	First British commando raid in Norway
MARCH 17	German is to be taught instead of English in schools from 1942 on
APRIL 23	All high school graduation celebrations prohibited
APRIL 28	"Books that damage national and social progress" prohibited
APRIL 29	Two of Norway's biggest holidays—May 1 and May 17—are decreed "normal working days"
MAY 30	Concerts must be approved; all song texts censored
AUGUST 2	Radios confiscated (exceptions for members of NS)
AUGUST 20	All Resistance in German-occupied countries is to be attributed to Communists; for every German killed in such cases, 50–100 hostages are to be executed
SEPTEMBER 26	Death penalty for attempting to "escape to enemy territory, or activities on behalf of the enemy"
DECEMBER 26-27	British commando raids against some coastal towns
DECEMBER 29	More German troops and ships sent to Norway

1942

JANUARY 5	Quisling signs National Youth Service law and Teachers Union law
JANUARY 7	Hitler issues *Nacht und Nebel* (Night and Fog) decree
JANUARY 24	The wearing of red hats (worn by students as "demonstration") prohibited
FEBRUARY	Executions in Ålesund and Televaag and reprisals for Norwegian Resistance
FEBRUARY 5	Teachers ordered to join the Teachers Union under NS control
MARCH 9	Labor and Athletics minister receives 5,000 letters from parents protesting Youth Service Act
MARCH 14	Dancing in public prohibited
MARCH–APRIL	Teachers reject new union; Quisling orders Norwegian police to arrest 1,100 teachers, 500 of whom are sent to forced labor camps in northern Norway
APRIL 5	Churches filled to capacity to hear sermon on "The Foundation of the Church"; most pastors resign
MAY 5	High school students to be called up for labor service
AUGUST 3	King's birthday; "illegal" flowers sold; over 200 arrested in Oslo for carrying flowers
SEPTEMBER 16	"Look to Norway" speech by U.S. President Franklin D. Roosevelt

OCTOBER 12	Terboven institutes death penalty for listening to radio, reading illegal newspapers, or possessing anti-German literature
OCTOBER–NOVEMBER	Jewish men, then women and children, arrested
NOVEMBER	Teachers who had been exiled to forced labor return home
DECEMBER–FEBRUARY 1943	760 Norwegian Jews sent to Auschwitz concentration camp

1943

FEBRUARY	Germans defeated at Stalingrad—a psychological turning point of the war
FEBRUARY 22	National Labor Act: all men ages 18–55 and all women ages 21–40 to register
FEBRUARY 28	Sabotage of Norsk Hydro "heavy water" plant, slowing work on possible German nuclear bomb
MARCH 25	New National Labor Act: all "healthy Norwegian youths to register"
NOVEMBER 30	1,200 university students arrested, 650 deported to prisons in Germany

1944

| JUNE 6 | D-day: Allied troops land at Normandy |
| SEPTEMBER | Finland surrenders to Russia; Germans retreat to Norway, use scorched-earth tactics in Finnmark (northern Norway) |

Timeline, 1940–1945

WINTER 1944-45	Harshest winter of the war; severe food shortages

1945

MAY 5-7	Germans capitulate in northwest Germany, Denmark, the Netherlands, and France
MAY 7	German surrender in Norway
MAY 8	Church bells rung for full hour at 3:00 P.M.
JUNE 7	King Haakon returns to Oslo, five years to the day he departed

Read On!

The following four books for young readers are wonderful stories about brave young people in Nazi-occupied Norway (and Denmark). Many fascinating stories can also be found at www.wwiinorge.com.

Casanova, Mary. *The Klipfish Code.* Boston: Houghton Mifflin, 1997.

Fuller, William, with Jack Haines. *Reckless Courage; The True Story of a Norwegian Boy Under Nazi Rule.* Marion, Mass.: Taber Hall Press, 2004.

Lowry, Lois. *Number the Stars.* Boston: Houghton Mifflin, 1989. (Denmark)

McSwigan, Marie. *Snow Treasure.* New York: Dutton, 1942.

Selected Bibliography

*Recommended for further reading or for advanced readers.

BOOKS

Adamson, Hans Christian, and Per Klem. *Blood on the Midnight Sun*. New York: Norton, 1964.

Astrup, Helen, and B. L. Jacot. *Oslo Intrigue: A Woman's Memoir of the Norwegian Resistance*. New York: McGraw-Hill, 1954.

Baden-Powell, Dorothy. *Pimpernel Gold: How Norway Foiled the Nazis*. New York: St. Martin's, 1978.

* Bartoletti, Susan Campbell. *Hitler Youth: Growing Up in Hitler's Shadow*. New York: Scholastic, 2005.

Berman, Irene Levin. *We Are Going to Pick Potatoes: Norway and the Holocaust—The Untold Story*. Lanham, Md.: Hamilton Books, 2010.

Broch, Theodor. *The Mountains Wait*. St. Paul, Minn.: Webb Book Publishing, 1942.

Cohen, Maynard H. *A Stand Against Tyranny: Norway's Physicians and the Nazis*. Detroit: Wayne State University Press, 1997.

Gardner, John. *On Moral Fiction*. New York: Basic Books, 1978.

* Haukelid, Knut. *Skis Against the Atom*. Minot, N. Dak.: North American Heritage Press, 1989.

Selected Bibliography

Hoye, Bjarne, and Trygve Ager. *The Fight of the Norwegian Church Against Nazism*. New York: Macmillan, 1943.

* Ippisch, Hanneke. *Sky*. New York: Simon and Schuster, 1996.

Nielsen, Thomas. *Inside Fortress Norway: Bjorn West— Norwegian Guerilla Base, 1944–1945*. Manhattan, Kans.: Sunflower University Press, 2000.

Petrow, Richard. *The Bitter Years: The Invasion and Occupation of Denmark and Norway, April 1940–May 1945*. New York: Morrow, 1974.

Riste, Olav, and Gerit Nokleby. *Norway 1940–45: The Resistance Movement*. Oslo, Norway: Tano, 1986.

Scott, Astrid Karlsen. *Silent Patriot: Norway's Most Highly Decorated WWII Soldier and Secret Agent*. Olympia, Wash.: Nordic Spirit, 1994.

* Sonsteby, Gunnar. *Report from #24*. Fort Lee, N.J.: Barricade Books, 1999.

Stokker, Kathleen. *Folklore Fights the Nazis: Humor in Occupied Norway, 1940–1945*: Madison, Wisc.: University of Wisconsin Press, 1995, 1997.

Terdal, Leif. *Our Escape from Nazi-Occupied Norway: Norwegian Resistance to Nazism*. Victoria, B.C.: Trafford Publishing, 2008.

OTHER SOURCES

Interviews with Erling Storrusten and Gunnar Garbo. Oslo, Norway. March 2011.

Norway's Resistance Museum (Norges Hjemmefronten Museum), Oslo Mil/Akershus, Oslo, Norway.

NOTES ON SPECIFIC REFERENCES IN THE TEXT

There are a great many more words in the English language than there are in Norwegian. Hence, translations from Norwegian into English can vary widely, depending on how the translator chooses to interpret the words. In the case of the Scharffenberg quotation accompanying the section "1945," I selected from among a variety of translated versions to offer the version easiest for young readers to comprehend.

The version of Odin drinking at Mimir's well is found in John Gardner's book, *On Moral Fiction.*

The episode of the prisoners eating turf and horse manure is based on real events as related by William Fuller and Jack Haines in their book *Reckless Courage.*

Acknowledgments

irst and foremost, I would like to express my heart-felt gratitude to Erling and Aase-Berit Storrusten for generously sharing the story of their experiences during the Occupation. I also want to thank Gunnar Garbo for sharing his poignant and powerful story. And thanks to the many Norwegians who steered me to points of interest, and to all the people who told me their stories of courage, hope, and grace. *Tusen takk!*

Thanks also to Geoff and Else Ward for the wealth of stories that can be found on their website www.wwiinorge. com. The stories kept me transfixed while the sun set, the light faded, and dinnertime came and went—and still I couldn't stop reading. Thank you for collecting and sharing them.

Mange tusen takk to Johan Bakken, Mette Breder, and Lise Lunge-Larsen for help with translations and Norwegian minutiae; my stellar critique group and others who read all or parts of the manuscript, especially Pasha Kahn, soccer and espionage adviser; illustrator Yuko Shimizu; garrison cartographer Ann Gumpper; and (secret) agent Steve Fraser.

Also a shout-out to Kathleen Stokker for her excellent

book *Folklore Fights the Nazis,* from which I freely borrowed, especially the jokes. *Takk for vitsene.*

To my patient and helpful husband, our brilliant children, and our Norwegian "son," Arne Christian Sivertsen (exchange student, 2000–2001), who was an enthusiastic companion on my research (and our skiing) trip to Norway, *takk.*

And, finally, a mountainous thank-you to everyone at Amulet/Abrams who worked on this book: Jim Armstrong, Chad Beckerman, Sara Corbett, Laura Mihalick, Jason Wells, and everyone else from that crazy-wonderful bunch who had a hand in it, most especially Howard Reeves, without whom this story would have been but a mere shadow.

About the Author

Margi Preus is an acclaimed children's book author and playwright whose first novel, *Heart of a Samurai*, earned a 2011 Newbery Honor award. She lives in Duluth, Minnesota. Visit her online at www.margipreus.com.

This book was designed by Chad W. Beckerman and Sara Corbett. The text in this book is set in Melior, a typeface designed in 1952 by Hermann Zapf, one of the twentieth century's most important type designers.

The typeface used on the cover is Blackball. Blackball was designed in 2009 by Dave Rowland, and it is based on traditional fraktur type.

The cover illustration is by Yuko Shimizu.

This book was printed and bound by R. R. Donnelley in Crawfordsville, Indiana. Its production was overseen by Alison Gervais.